VIEW OF A REMOTE COUNTRY

VIEW OF A REMOTE COUNTRY

KAREN TRAVISS

Collected short stories from 1999 to 2003

DEDICATION

For Sean Baggaley, fellow *One Step Beyond* workshopper, for unstinting technical support and generally being an all-round good egg.

This is a work of fiction. All the characters, organizations, companies, locations, countries, objects, situations, and events portrayed in this novel are either products of the author's imagination or are used fictitiously. Any resemblance to people living or dead is coincidental.

All rights reserved. Except for the use in any review, the reproduction or utilization of this work in whole or in part in any form by any electronic, mechanical or other means is forbidden without the express permission of the author.

Copyright 2014 by Karen Traviss

All rights reserved.

Published by Karen Traviss
www.karentraviss.com

ISBN-13: 978-1500551360
ISBN-10: 1500551368

CONTENTS

FOREWORD

RETURN STORES — Page 3

SUITABLE FOR THE ORIENT — Page 19

DEATH, TAXES, AND MACKEREL — Page 39

EVIDENCE — Page 51

AN OPEN PRISON — Page 65

CHOCOLATE KINGS — Page 79

A SLICE AT A TIME — Page 87

STRINGS — Page 101

VIEW OF A REMOTE COUNTRY — Page 119

THE MAN WHO DID NOTHING — Page 135

DOES HE TAKE BLOOD? — Page 159

THE LAST PENNY — Page 171

ORCHIDS — Page 185

FOREWORD

Before the glaciers melted, short fiction magazines walked the Earth. I know, because I was there. Well, okay, some have survived to the present day, but they're much smaller and less influential now, a T Rex reduced to a sparrow, and many others have gone the way of the passenger pigeon.

This is the remote country; short stories I wrote for magazines years ago and haven't glanced at since. I barely recall writing most of them, and I admit they came as a surprise to me, as unfamiliar as if a stranger had written them.

But the roots of my novels lie in them somewhere. Between 1998 and 2002, I wrote a flurry of these shorts while I was gearing up to escape the corporate world for a career as a full-time novelist. The stories ended up in a number of magazines such as *Asimov's* and the now-defunct *Realms of Fantasy*. What you see in these pages is the result of that, a mix of SF and fantasy, and the last that I wrote before novels and commissioned fiction took over my working day.

This anthology isn't the complete collection, only the surviving manuscripts. If I recover any more of them, I'll add them and re-issue this book. The stories aren't in date order, just arranged for variety, so they all carry their date of publication and an explanatory note. None have been re-edited – that struck me as cheating – but I've standardised them throughout to UK spelling, although they were almost all published in US English.

Many were written as exercises at the Clarion East workshop held at Michigan State University in the summer of 2000, but a few were written a couple of years earlier for the UK's *One Step Beyond* workshop in 1998. Workshops gave me the opportunity to experiment with point-of-view, genre, language, and structure, but as I'm someone who hates seeing any effort go to waste, I later sold the resulting stories to magazines. Some stories have been overtaken by the real world, an occupational hazard for SF authors. One of the older ones, *The Last Penny*, turned out to be more predictive than I could have imagined, and not in a good way.

So why assemble these stories now? I kept getting requests for a collection from readers who couldn't find the magazines years later, but for the writers among you, or for anyone who's curious about how writers evolve, these stories are a snapshot of the ideas I was kicking around in those days, the aliens I was trying out for size, and the narrator perspectives I test-drove before I worked out my approach to novel-length work. In the end, first person point-of-view went in the bin and has never appeared in any novel except for prologues. Present tense went the same way, as did fantasy and humour. In the end I opted to write military fiction instead, and my books have followed a different evolutionary path although the underlying themes of identity and the moral dilemmas of technology remain.

Anyway, I hope you enjoy them. And if you haven't read any of my novels yet, you can have fun spotting the components from these shorts that were eventually recycled in longer works.

Karen Traviss
July 2014

RETURN STORES

(First published in *Realms of Fantasy*, February 2003.)

Today, I'm just a madman blowing a dented brass bugle while the street where my grandfather lived in is razed to the ground.

It's amazing how fast they can knock down a terrace of houses. First the crane swings the ball at the end house. You see the walls peel away, and the floors collapse, leaving the party wall. It's like a sheet from a cardboard doll's house, the sort you fold and slot together: there's pink emulsion paint marking where the bathroom was, and blue Georgian stripe wallpaper in the bedroom, but no walls separating them, just a torn line where the stud partitions were. Maybe you can slot it all back together again somehow.

I give the bugle another strangled blast. It's much harder than you'd think to get a brass instrument to make a noise. The demolition team glance at me from time to time, but they probably can't hear it.

The sound isn't for them, anyway. It's for the house, the last one left in the row.

#

Ten years ago, when my grandfather died, he left me his

home.

When I opened the cupboard, the smell of a lifetime ago hit me; oily, musty and faintly bitter at the back of my throat. I reached out to touch the workman's coat that I knew had to be hanging there. I knew it would feel slightly damp under my fingers, and that it would carry the dark patina of graphite grease.

I clutched at air. The cupboard was empty, except for the heritage of its dockyard smell.

"Your grandfather didn't do much to this house, Mr Hollis," said the solicitor. He kept looking at his watch: he obviously had better-paying clients than students like me to attend to. "But property prices round here are going up, and you can probably get an improvement grant from the council. So, all in all, not a bad inheritance."

A shabby two-up, two-down flat fronted terraced house with an outside toilet and no central heating. It was a scene from one of those time-warp programmes where they made people live in the 1940s for a month without fridges and unlimited hot water. But to a student like me it was a potential palace, somewhere I could be independent and have parties without worrying about rent, or my mother complaining about the spilled beer and the noise.

Granddad's furniture was still there, war-time utility style, polished so many times the varnish was worn through on the edges. A time-speckled mirror with green faceted glass edges still hung above the tiny gas fire, and there were a couple of amateur paintings of warships hanging on the wall. Granddad had been a welder in the dockyard and the navy had been his life right up to the time he lost his job.

Mum said he was sacked for pilfering and that he'd never got over the shame of it. I knew that: when he'd had a glass of beer or whisky at Christmas, he'd go quiet and miserable and then talk about the dockyard and how he would clear his name. That seemed terribly important, because his name was also my name, Arthur, although I never told kids at school what the A after Mark was for. My mother would say: "Come on, Dad, it's all history now." But it wasn't over for him, not at all. Once, just once, he took me up a ladder to the attic where he showed me a battered brass bugle that he said would prove he was innocent. When I asked Mum about it she said that grown-ups often said stupid things when they'd had a drink.

But today I was that kid again, hiding in the coats and waiting for Granddad to find me. His shirt, his coat, everything he wore at work was speckled with tiny weld burns. At Christmas dinner when I was six, I remembered him crying and making Mum embarrassed when he rambled on about the injustice of being sacked and how they had stabbed him in the back. I thought he had to be brave, because he was just like the heroes in films who got stabbed but went on fighting. And I decided there and then that bosses had to be very bad people to stab my Granddad and that I'd never, ever work for one.

#

Up in the attic, I found half-used cans of paint, more newspapers than I had ever seen in my life, and a ball of string made up of different lengths and colours knotted neatly together. I remembered lots of balls like that. But there was also a boxed dinner service and an old blue suitcase.

Granddad tended to hoard things, my Mum said, but they were *useful* things. Paper – well, you could do a lot with old newsprint. And string. "You'll be glad of that one day," he'd say, and knot another rescued length on to the last. It was typical of people who'd lived through the war and rationing, Mum said. They never got out the habit of saving what they could.

The blue suitcase was the last thing I opened, after I had heaved all the other stuff I couldn't find a use for into someone else's rubbish skip further along the road. It was a long job, waiting until it got dark and then taking the stuff out a bag at a time. I didn't know then how you went about hiring a skip, and I didn't think it was wrong to use something that someone else had paid for. I still can't remember exactly when my attitude to what was right and proper changed, but it did.

I put the suitcase on the kitchen table and stared at it for a while, almost embarrassed to open it. It was Granddad's. It was personal. But I did. The rusty catches snapped open, and when I lifted the lid I inhaled old newspaper, leather and mildew. There were documents in a tattered manila envelope that was sueded from frequent handling, cracked photographs in varying tones of brown and grey, a couple of tally bands from sailors' caps, and the old bugle he'd shown me that one Christmas.

The documents were insurance policies and receipts long out of date. I spent more time looking at the photographs. Warships with men standing in front of them, self-conscious men, some of them with those thin little hand-rolled cigarettes Granddad called "ticklers". It was a matter of pride to be able to roll them with just one hand, he said.

I remembered that quite suddenly. He was a dockyardman – pronounced locally as *docky-ardman*. Docky-ardmen called their tea kitty a *tea boat* and had a language all their own. These pictures showed docky-ardmen paused at work, welders, riggers, shipwrights, all trades a man could be proud of. Pencilled on the backs of the prints were notes – not in Granddad's hand – like *Repairing Caisson No 4* and *Illustrious, North Corner*. And there were pictures of a tide of men on bicycles streaming out of the dockyard gates, hundreds of them, so many that nobody on bike, on foot or even in a car could have made headway against that flow.

It had once been the biggest industrial complex in Europe. Maybe that was one of the reasons Granddad had loved it so much; it was a nation in its own right with a clear sense of what it was there for, and every man a citizen. I picked up one of the pictures that seemed more recent. It was a retirement presentation, but not Granddad's of course, although he was in the picture. The men with him were all posed around another man holding a framed certificate. When I turned it over, the names were written on the back, and this time the notes were Granddad's handwriting.

L-R – *Nobby Clark, Dusty Miller, Tugg Wilson.* All those daft nicknames: I never understood why they needed to rename people, but the civilians did it just as the navy did, perhaps aping their uniformed masters. Or perhaps it was the industrial version of a tribal initiation, where you were cleansed of your mundane name to reinforce your passage into another world, the world of steel ships. Did they take Granddad's name from him to show he had been fired, like breaking a disgraced officer's sword? It made me inexplicably sad. I knew I would never need to write my friends' names on the backs of their photographs. I'd remember them perfectly.

There were no pictures of the family or Grandma in the case. In fact, I never found any in the house at all.

I picked up the bugle and peered down into its depths, then held it to my lips and tried half-heartedly to blow a note. I was afraid I'd wake up the whole terrace. But I couldn't get a sound from it. I tried a little harder, and harder still, and even when I started to feel giddy from blowing the thing I still couldn't get more than a strangled raspberry from it. I put it on the draining board, and wrote *brass polish* on the shopping list I'd stuck on the side of one of the cabinets. I'd clean the bugle up.

Sometime, too, I thought, I'd see if Nobby or Tugg or Dusty or any of the others in that retirement picture were still around. I felt I needed to talk to people who knew a Granddad that the family didn't.

#

I imagined I would have a job to trace people from so long ago. I was wrong. The librarian tapped at her keyboard, sending lists scrolling down her screen and then printed me off details of places I could start. There were ex-dockyard associations, the dockyard historical society and even a "where are they now" column in the local paper.

"You know, you could even just ask round the area," she said. "This might look like a city but it's really a big village. People don't move far from here. Some people have never even been off the island. We stay, and it's just the itinerant population that comes and goes."

"Navy and students?" I said.

"Mainly students now."

She meant me, I realised, and it was the first time it had struck me that I didn't sound local. I'd had a middle class education and I didn't say "wont" and "int" any longer. But the idea of never leaving the city – the island – seemed amazing to my generation. I wanted out. I was going to qualify as a civil engineer and I was going to work for myself, not for bosses or foremen like Granddad did. I had all these financial rationalisations about the benefits of self-employment, but being back in his house reminded me of my real motivation. Bosses stabbed you. Bosses could take away your job, your whole identity, even your sanity, and no bugger was going to do to me what they had done to Granddad.

I polished the bugle with oily wads of DuraGlit. It took some time to bring up the lustre, and I was inexplicably pleased with myself when I did. Then I held it to my lips. The taste was awful. I should have washed the mouthpiece off first, so as an afterthought I ran it under the tap and dried it on the tea-towel, cherishing a moment of rebellion because Mum said tea-towels were only for plates and cutlery. But this was my house: I could be a slob here if I pleased.

Nobody was there to see me. I felt I was blushing anyway. *Stupid thing to do...* I gave the bugle a cautious puff, then a more determined blow with my lips hard together.

The note startled me. It was pure and unwavering, not an agonised *tharrpp*, and it made my ears ring. The mirror over the fire shivered slightly.

Granddad, muttering about his disgrace, and Mum crying in the kitchen after Dad shouted at her and said it was time the silly old sod shut up about it. Granddad worked as a brewery drayman for years after he left the Yard, Mum said: he made lots of friends and did well, but I never remembered any of that. He never got over the Yard. So neither would I. I gave the bugle a few more blasts and surprised myself by managing to hold a long, pure note for what seemed like eternity.

This time the two spent six-inch brass shell cases standing on the mantelpiece rattled slightly on their bases. I decided to put the bugle away for a while.

In the evenings after lectures, I started looking for the dockyard associations. In a couple of weeks I was being entertained modestly in back-room bars by old boys who talked the foreign language of my Granddad, the language of *tiffs* and *tiddly jobs* and *parting brass rags*.

Inside a month, I'd found some of Granddad's old mates. There I go again. I almost called them *colleagues*.

#

Nobby and Dusty drank pints of bitter top, one of those old men's tastes I hadn't acquired, a glass slightly short of a pint of bitter with a shot of barley wine added for impact. I was still a lager man in those days. It was long before I affected a taste for Pinot Noir and Waitrose Good Ordinary Claret. The bar was small and the walls were covered with that Victorian-style textured paper you could paint over a hundred times and still see the embossed design. Its latest incarnation was chocolate brown gloss, possibly because there was so much smoke in the bar that any other colour would have surrendered to brown anyway.

"We never lost touch with Janner," Dusty said. It was the first time I had heard his nickname: his real name was Arthur. "I mean, it was a terrible thing in them days, to be sacked for thieving, but he was straight as a die and we never believed it." He took his baccy tin from his jacket and began assembling a cigarette, rolling it with one hand: and yes, it was a skill to behold. "It did get to him, though. There was the bugle thing."

Nobby nodded, and coughed impressively. "Yeah, *Return Stores*. We thought he was off his rocker then, but it was harmless enough."

Bugle? Bugles weren't something that cropped up that often, not in the life I was leading, and I had one and here we were talking about it. "What about the bugle?" I said.

"Daft dockyard legend." Nobby hacked noisily again, and Dusty's tickler was already ashes. "Return Stores. It was supposed to be a bugle call, from when prisoners worked in the Yard and the army – not the navy, son, this was an army garrison as well as a port – the army watched over them, and at the end of the day the bugler would play Return Stores to let them know it was time to take their tools and doings back to the stores. So on Judgement Day, *Return Stores* would be sounded, and all the stuff that had been nicked over the years from the dockyard and found its way into people's homes would rise up and march back to the Yard. And 'cos so much had been nicked over the centuries, the whole city would collapse when the stuff marched off."

"Rabbit," I said. It was one of the words I remembered Granddad using: rabbit. It was Yard slang for materials stolen from the yard, or anything made out of them. As a boy I really thought dockyardmen took home real rabbits under their diesel-scented coats.

"That's it, son. Rabbit." Nobby laughed and it started him coughing again. "And they really *was* real rabbits, once, when the Yard covered part of the Common."

My skin prickled. I dismissed a thought that he might have read my memories. I suppose all kids thought rabbits were real: and I once thought Granddad really had been stabbed in the back. "I found a bugle in his attic," I said.

"Daft sod was convinced he'd blow it some day, just to prove his house didn't fall down and so it wasn't full of stuff he'd nicked." He pronounced the contractions as "dint" and "wont". "I ask yer."

"So what does *Return Stores* sound like?"

"Haven't a clue, son. Nobody seems to. You could ask the

army. It's just a legend, anyway."

"So why did Granddad keep the bugle, then?" He hadn't been remotely musical, and he only kept *useful* things. "I know he was traumatised by the sacking, but surely not enough to develop an obsession."

Nobby looked at me as if I had spoken Latin to him. "He went a bit funny in the head after he had to leave the Yard. Never the same."

Kids don't notice the broad sweep of misery, just the detail. I knew Grandma got angry with him when we visited, and Mum said the sacking had "put a lot of strain" on everyone. But nobody died, and life carried on as normal in my self-centred kid's eyes, even if Granddad did cry when he wasn't supposed to.

I had a question about the bugle. "Where did he get it? Do you know?" If I imagined there would be a romantic explanation, I was wrong.

"Rabbit," said Nobby, and they all laughed. "Nicked it off some Booty when there was this drinking session. Now that *was* bloody daft, pilfering from a Marine."

My blameless Granddad, a thief after all. Part of me felt shudderingly sick, the part raised on Granddad the poor but honest working man, victim of management. The other part felt a sense of relief that I might not have family honour to satisfy.

But I liked Nobby. I wished Granddad were still here so I could buy him a pint of bitter top, too, and talk to him and understand him. All I had, though, was Nobby, and I sent him a Christmas card via the association every year after that.

As for Return Stores, I never did find anyone – army, navy or marines – who knew what the bugle call should sound like.

#

Four years later, after I had left university and no longer needed Granddad's house, I sold it. There was nothing of him left there, and I wanted it far behind the current *me* that was now making a living as construction engineer. I was self-employed, free of stabbing bosses. Even if I faced gaps between contracts, they still couldn't take my profession from me, nor the rabbited bugle, nor the photographs.

I took them with me too, with my identity. I put them in a box and forgot them twice for eight years. When I moved house – twice, once when I lost my contract – I rediscovered them and took them out and thought about Granddad. I was old enough to appreciate that a job was who you were, and that losing it unfairly really hurt. Then I forgot about them again. I forgot because I had another contract with a big civil engineering company and a life and I felt secure enough at work to think about getting married.

I forgot about the bugle, right up to the time the doctor told Mum she had stomach cancer.

Visiting her in hospital meant a long drive down south. Up to then, I had thought I had time to come to terms with it. But it was a late diagnosis. She was shrunken in that big awkward hospital bed, a scrap of someone I used to know, silenced by drugs and full of tubes. She looked like a stranger. If I'd thought living a long way from home was a way of blunting the impact of family death, I was wrong.

I managed to fit in four visits before she died. One Saturday evening, while I was sitting beside her bed and watching the occasional nurse wander in and out of the ward, she stirred.

"I was thinking about Dad," she said, her voice distorted by the cancer and the nasogastric tube.

Still the self-centred kid, I thought she meant my father, who'd left four years ago. I started thinking of ways to find the bastard and get him here, if that was what she wanted. Then I realised she meant her own father, Granddad.

"Were you, Mum?"

"He was so upset."

"About what?"

"Being sacked. The kids in my class didn't let me forget it. Thief. *Thief.*"

"It's okay, Mum," I said. "Nobody believed it anyway. Don't you worry about that now."

"He wanted to prove it," she said. "That trumpet thing."

They were near enough the last words she ever spoke. Call me stupid, but it's amazing how imperative dying words can be compared to every plea and order and demand from the living. I owed it one last try.

#

The naval base authorities (it was no longer a dockyard by then, stripped of its rank in the defence cuts) were less than helpful. They couldn't go into an industrial case so many years in the past, they said, and anyway they probably couldn't find the records, and they were *very sorry*. The official I spoke to on the phone had the tone of voice of a man revealing nothing for fear of legal action rather than one wary of divulging state secrets, almost deferential. I had developed an effective middle-class tone of outraged insistence that wore down bosses and would have made Granddad proud.

But they still couldn't help. I spent months harrying them, and months in the central library going back through newspapers and microfiche, but it yielded nothing. I had done all I could. At least I thought I had, right up until the autumn that year when I got a letter from Nobby.

His handwriting was careful and remarkably ornate for a plain man, all extravagant wobbly loops. They were demolishing the houses, he said. Did I want to come down south and see Janner's house – Granddad's house – one last time before they knocked it down?

Of course I did.

I arrived with the photographs, now filed neatly in an album, and the bugle. Nobby still had a hacking cough, but the ticklers hadn't claimed him yet.

"What you doin' now, son?" he asked. "Still building them roads and towers?"

"I'm a consulting engineer now, in a partnership."

"Good to have a trade that's up in yer head like that, not like a job with yer hands." We drank in that same pub, and the walls were still brown gloss embossed. It might have been a new coat of brown, but I couldn't tell. "They've started knocking them down already, y'know. Half of Kassassin Street's gone."

"I brought Granddad's pictures. Like to have a look?" "

Nobby was entranced. He could name most of the men in the photographs and provided instant histories of them and the work they were pictured doing. I should have been comforted by the reminiscence, but it only served to remind me that Granddad had a life I could now only know through the recollections of his old mates.

"See you brought the bugle," he said.

I fumbled with the carrier bag. It didn't disguise the shape very well. "I wondered if you might like it as a keepsake," I lied.

Nobby laughed. "I don't have that much time to keep now," he said. "Or you could give it to the museum. Don't expect they'd worry how your Granddad got it."

"I suppose that's the irony. He did steal something."

"Janner wasn't the only bloke lifted for nicking stuff, son." His smoke-stained fingertips were like tan leather, as if he were gloved. He shook slightly while he rolled a tickler and had to steady it with a touch from his other hand. "It was an industry. Your old Granddad might have been the only one not at it, 'cept for the bugle of course. There was even a bloke who put Epsom salts in his sugar tin to stop his mates nicking it, only he forgot and had some himself." Nobby roared with laughter again. "Serves the tight sod right."

He was having trouble getting the lid back on his baccy tin and I reached out to do it for him. It surprised me that he let me. "Did you steal stuff?"

"A spanner or two. I knew a bloke who did his kitchen out all in crabfat grey, you know, warship paint, just 'cos he could. One even had that real gold paint off the royal yacht." He paused for a long swallow of bitter top, and I thought he might be finished. But he went on. "It was an art, getting stuff past the coppers on the gate, under your coat, whatever. They stopped you and searched you in the hut. Best I ever heard was the bike job, though. They never caught him."

"Go on."

"Bloke they thought was thieving. Every night at knocking off time, they'd stop him at the gate and he'd get off his pushbike and they'd turn him over. Nothing. Never found bugger all. Years later we heard he'd been nicking the bikes and riding 'em out the Yard."

"Is that an apocryphal tale?" I asked.

"What's that, then?"

"Like *Return Stores*. A yarn."

"Might be."

Nobby enjoyed the rest of his pint and then a couple more. I wished I'd heard these tales from Granddad. Now I was soaking up yarns from the last of a generation of men who would take their fables with them to the grave, because well-educated people like me hadn't seen them for the history they truly were. It was *my* history.

"Everything's got to have an end to it," he said. His tone was different now, almost gentle, as if he were afraid he'd hurt a child's feelings. "You should get it out of your system, now that the house is going."

"How?" I knew how. I'd just lost my nerve. "Any ideas?"

He nudged the carrier bag with his boot. "Blow that bloody thing and get it over with."

Perhaps he had a more sophisticated grasp of psychology than I imagined a working man was capable of. He was telling me I needed closure. If I did what Granddad had believed might prove he hadn't been a thief, the mind-magic might work.

I couldn't argue with that. It was better than living with that nagging at the back of my mind. I'd do it for Mum, but most of all I'd do it for myself and for Granddad.

"Would you come with me?" I asked. "If it works, if I blow the bugle and the house doesn't fall down, I think

Granddad would want one of his mates to see the proof." And we laughed as if it were a bad joke, but we *knew* it was irrational and why we were really doing it. We both had to put it to rest. Well, I did. Nobby was just being supportive like a real Granddad.

The contractor demolishing the terrace was as helpful as a street artist inviting people to watch him paint. They would probably get round to the houses the day after tomorrow, and it was *no problem at all* for me to watch as long as I observed safety regulations, and seeing I was an *engineer* I would know all about those things.

Granddad's house stood in two facing terraces of boarded-up properties preparing to make way for a new development of one-bedroom apartments. The city had always been packed tight, trying to sprawl in its corset of an island. Nobby and I stood on the corner of the street for a long time and watched the diggers and cranes coming to life.

I always carried hard hats in my car, the smart green and white ones bearing the name Butcher Gascoine and Hollis. *See, Granddad, I made it: a partner. No bosses for me.* Nobby and I put them on and moved closer to the demolition.

I still had the bugle in the Waitrose carrier bag, as befitted the upwardly mobile, and it embarrassed me to take it out. Then, suddenly, it didn't. I held it to my lips.

I paused and looked at Nobby. "I still haven't a clue what *Return Stores* should sound like," I said.

"Nobody does, son," he said, squinting through spiralling wisps of cigarette smoke. "Just do what comes into your head."

I put the bugle to my lips. Fall, Jericho; fall, houses built from rabbit; fall, all those kitchens painted crabfat grey. It was time to march home to the yard.

#

Nobby nudges me, and points to a short section of pipe rolling slowly down the slight incline of the pavement. It comes to a halt. "I know where that's going," he says, and roars with laughter.

But Granddad's house is still standing. They're having another go at it. One of the demolition crew is cursing about "fucking metal RSJs" but I know it's not the rolled steel joists standing against the onslaught.

It's the *house*. It's telling everyone it was built and furnished fair and square, with nothing stolen or filched or sneaked through the dockyard gates. For a few private minutes, it vindicates my grandfather. Nobby has seen the house stand alone, and so have I.

And I know those houses were never built with rolled steel joists.

Nobby waves goodbye. I slip the bugle into the carrier bag and start walking towards the sea front. I'm taking it to the museum, where they won't mind that it's *rabbit*. Perhaps they can knock the dents out of the bugle and keep a shine on it. Perhaps, one day, they'll even find someone who knows how to play *Return Stores*.

SUITABLE FOR THE ORIENT

(First published in *Asimov's*, February 2003. Honourable mention, Year's Best Science Fiction #21. Written as an exercise at Clarion East Workshop, 2000. My only memory of this was the excellent Greg Frost, our tutor, reading it in a Clouseau accent because of the word "minkies.")

In a place where there are no humans, one must strive to be human.

(Rabbi Hillel)

I lost another patient this morning.

The family took the body away, and I spent an hour trying to clean the surgery. Now I had a fibre cup of vodka and cold black coffee in my hand; and every time I raised it I could smell the sulphur and strawberry odour of aliens on my fingers, even though I'd worn gloves and scrubbed my nails clean with a stiff brush until my cuticles bled. The minkies' body fluids were amazingly persistent.

I was drunk with Bob the maintenance man, as I often was on Friday nights, both of us crammed in his four square meter office so close to the generators that the vibration made the surface of my drink shiver if I put the cup on his desk. And I mean that I was drunk, not just that I was drinking, although that was obviously true as well.

Bob said he saved his doctor jokes for me because I needed to see the lighter side of my calling. Fresh jokes were in short supply in an isolated colony ten light years from home: we didn't meet many new people.

"So the guy asks who he is, and St Peter says, 'That's God playing doctor.'" Bob tapped my knee with a length of foam insulation tube. I was sitting on his locked tool cabinet. "Good one, eh, doc?"

"Heard it. And it was a white coat, not green."

"You shouldn't let it get you down, Frank."

I must have been staring into mid-distance. "And what if this is the pinnacle of my career?"

"I meant the minkies. They just die, y'know."

"Not the first time I've had an alien die on me," I said, and wished I had been caught feeling compassion instead of self-pity.

I drank with Bob because I wanted to. We were both mid-thirties and going nowhere. Stagnation was made more comfortable because someone on-base had worked out how to bypass the beer rations and acquire illicit alcohol. But they never thought of making a good mixer to go with it, so we settled for coffee and a touch of sweetener to pretend we were downing Black Russians.

"You could go back to Earth for a hospital job," Bob said.

"My training's already twenty-five years out of date before I step on the shuttle."

"Can't you retrain?"

"What's the point?"

I found out that I was good only for minor medicine when I pulled my file as a final year medical student. Someone had coded "SFTO" on the header. Medics were notorious for cryptic codes on files. It was a long time before I found out what SFTO meant, but I did, and it meant SUITABLE FOR

THE ORIENT. It was an old, old saying from the days of the British Empire, when the colonial civil service sent barely competent doctors to Asia and India – the orient – because it didn't matter if they killed the natives. The really good doctors attended white men.

So I was suitable for an orient which was a colony and support base on Hera, a month's subjective-time flight from earth but actually ten years distant. No one cared if I couldn't save aliens and it wasn't my job to try too hard.

The minkies turned up at my infirmary a couple of times a month, usually haemorrhaging from a puncture wound or laceration. Sometimes I got adults clutching a dehydrated infant. I would try to stop the haemorrhage manually, or get some distilled water into them. That was all I could do, apart from trying to remove their sickly odour. They accepted the deaths with a humming sound. Some people responded instinctively to the howls of distressed animals, but that mournful, resigned *mmmmmm* with its gradually falling note always stirred a shared misery in me.

I had known gifted colleagues who would have known intuitively how to save them, I was sure of that. But not me. And we were too busy trying to give the human colony a foothold to worry about the locals. The study of the minkies was left to the hobbyists to tackle in their spare time. Colony life was uncertain, and the priority was to survive, not to publish research papers.

There were more minkies around that year than I'd seen in the previous four that I'd been on-base. I found them appealing: and they were completely un-simian. I really never liked monkeys, not since my parents had taken me to see various species in a wildlife park and I had sat in the car in terror while baboons ripped off wing mirrors and slapped their horribly human palms on the windshield.

Minkies were a meter and a half tall fully grown, part elephant skin and part glossy fur, which made them look like luxury sloths with a bad case of mange. I have no idea who gave them the name but it made people laugh and reduced the aliens to the safe status of cartoons.

Some were light grey, and some were dark charcoal, almost black: and that fur really was mink-like. But there was no fashion in the making there. When they died in my surgery, as they usually did, the fur was the first part of them to start decomposing.

The part-time xenologists had been studying them for years, but it was slow going. These were not animals, and they made it clear with charging gestures that they didn't want to be observed unless it was on their terms. I admired the creatures for that. Unlike humans overtaken by a technologically advanced colonial power, minkies didn't want anything back from us. They left us alone. They were too preoccupied with fighting each other, and there seemed to be an endless supply of them ready to join the battle.

Derra Houlihan, the closest person we had to a xenologist, said it was all over food gathering rights, but all I knew was that the injured and sick had started to come to my clinics because the main medical centre in the settlement turned them away.

I didn't mind at first. I was there to treat the fit, young support personnel, and as any ship's doctor could tell you, young fit people just broke bones, drank themselves sick or caught STDs. It was basic doctoring, the sort even an SFTO medic like me could handle, so I had time on my hands. The minkies didn't complain about my lack of skill with needle samplers either.

The more the minkies turned up, though, the more they were reminding me that I wasn't fulfilling my mother's high expectations of my medical career. As a child I wished for siblings to divert her attention from me, and as a married man I prayed unsuccessfully for children for the same reason, but neither happened. I wondered if saving the occasional minkie would have placated her.

#

Colonists and support personnel didn't mix socially. We discouraged it, and so did they. The colonist mind-set was stable and familial, and the support personnel were all single status military or techs on five-year deployments. You couldn't sustain any sort of family relationship over a twenty-five year time differential, so it was a posting that attracted the young, the coerced or the alienated. There was a time when I kidded myself I was in the first category. The peacekeeping troops were mainly both young and coerced. What peace they were designed to keep we didn't know, but they did secure new areas, provide engineering muscle and round up those for whom even the modest ration of weak beer was a little too exciting.

It wasn't that the support team and colonists didn't try to bridge the gap. I had my share of morning appointments with pregnant colony girls who had been captivated by a well-filled peacekeeper's uniform, but I didn't do terminations. I sent the kids back to their own doctors. It wasn't my world and I wasn't going to make decisions for it. The colonists were here to be people, but we were only here to do a job.

The average day for a doctor on a frontier colonial planet didn't reflect the imagined glories of the Raj. We didn't sip brandy and sodas on the veranda as the sun set over the tea plantation, and there were no turbaned soda-wallahs attending to our every need. I spent nine hours out of the twenty-nine hour day in a cabin (this was originally navy territory, remember) that measured four meters by five and had no exterior window. My video screen was my view on the world. I didn't write letters home from my one-piece moulded desk as in the recruitment ads because my father was long dead and I knew my mother probably was as well.

She was sixty three when I left Earth and since I'd been here for four years and six months, plus ten years time dilation, I stopped writing the first time I didn't receive one of her disappointed replies to my ethermails.

Bob told me I ought to request official confirmation but I couldn't face ten years waiting to be told she was fine and then start the cycle over again. I pronounced her dead, like a doctor should.

I did keep relative Earth time on my organizer screen, though. I had savings and investments back there to consider, and for people away for decades at a time, calculating compound interest was a major hobby. But I didn't want to be one of those homesick time-displaced types who dreamed of going back and then found they were so far out of real-time that they only had other unemployable space ex-pats to talk to. Was there an alternative? I hadn't worked that out yet. I kept in slow touch with my bank just in case.

The other twenty hours of the day, I held clinics, recorded health data for researchers and loafed around. I read a lot. I estimated I spent two and a half hours a day eating, all within an optimum nutritional profile. It was too easy to eat for recreation and at 1.2 Earth gravity, carrying extra weight on Hera was left you breathless and arthritic, as Bob found out the hard way.

I also took an hour a day to walk round the country surrounding the base. I liked the reed beds best, especially in the frost. Tiny flying creatures with white fur darted through the plants and I could sit in the grass with a flask of vodka and coffee and pretend they were birds, and that the plants were just what they appeared to be.

We were on the coast of a landmass near the southern pole, far from the equatorial zones where the daytime temperature topped 60 degrees. On a sunny day it reminded me of New Zealand.

I wondered if I would ever visit Auckland again.

#

After four years I could understand some minkie gestures and language well. They were expressive patients so I knew most of the code for levels of distress, parts of their anatomy and supplication, but that was where it ended. The amateur alien-watchers were still arguing, when other duties permitted, over whether they had true language: they thought minkies were more intelligent than chimps but less smart than Neanderthals, although opinions varied.

Without my colleagues' academic background, I was free to make the unscientific assumption that minkies were pretty clever. They'd found a medic, they could make me understand what they wanted, and they didn't like being videoed. I could respect all that.

Minkies were only communal when they needed to be. I'd see them mainly on their own, or carrying youngsters, although they formed groups to pick the grassland clean of food and, of course, to kill each other. I only saw greys with greys and blacks with blacks, so the conclusion I drew was immediate: there were at least two tribes. But this morning I found three adult blacks at the surgery door that opened onto the main compound. They were carrying another adult, a grey.

It had a chest wound. That wasn't unusual. They made their *ahk-ahk-ahk* noise of panic when I gloved up, and they tried to help me lift it on to the examination couch, which was a little high for them. It was dead as far as I could tell. It stank of sulphur and fruit, and its beautiful silver fur dragged like carpet under my gloves as it began degrading.

"Dead," I said. I made two closed fists against my chest as best I could and made a long sighing noise. "Dead. I'm very sorry."

They looked at me, pupils snapping from wide open to pinpricks, but they didn't start their usual quiet humming. They just looked and then they began flinging their arms wide. It was when I turned the body over that I began to realize what was different today.

There was an exit wound the size of a walnut. Minkie weapons were spears and clubs and didn't do that sort of damage. It was a ballistic round. I had seen an accidental weapon discharge injury to a soldier's foot around eighteen months ago, and it looked just like that.

I gestured to them to sit down on the floor and I peeled

my gloves off so I wouldn't get the smell on my comms touch-pad. I called the base commander direct, because doctors could do that sort of thing, even second-rate ones like me.

#

"I'll start an investigation," Commander Da Silva said. I didn't know if she had been that close to minkies before, but she kept her gaze on them the whole time. I interpreted their continuous arm waving as anger. "If it's one of my personnel, they'll be damned sorry."

How could I explain that to the minkies? I couldn't wait for a linguist to show up, even if they could handle this situation. I tried the sorrow sign, hunching into a ball and humming, so I had either apologized or told them I too was grieving. They moved towards the door, but as it opened for them one turned back and made a final anger gesture.

"I haven't seen them like that before," I said. "I'd say they were really angry."

Da Silva was rubbing her forehead with her fingers as if she were massaging away a headache. "Just as well they only have sticks and stones."

"You *are* going to investigate, aren't you?"

"Hey, I don't tolerate any of my people taking pot shots at the natives."

"It has to be one of yours, though. Have you got forensic facilities or do we need to contact HQ?"

Her grey hair was sticking up where she'd been rubbing. "It won't be that hard. Most of the troops here are from engineer regiments. That wound's from a sniper's weapon. It's down to one of fifty infantry personnel, and the military police can shake that one out with good old fashioned redcap persistence."

"I hope they've not started hunting them. It's boring out here for combat troops."

"Maybe the minkies were raiding crops." But she shook

her head sadly. "No, they don't do that, do they? They leave us alone. They're good little aliens."

"You'll let me know?"

"Of course."

I knew she would. Some people thought the military were savages under their polite formality. But I was always heartened by how their human decency held out long after civilians had started tearing their neighbours apart. You noticed that sort of thing in federal Europe.

Da Silva sent me a message three days later. One of the infantrymen had hired his rifle out to a seventeen-year-old colonist for a bottle of vodka. It was a civilian matter now, and the soldier was being shipped back to HQ for court martial.

He was facing five years' imprisonment. The colonists, on the other hand, decided to take no action against the youngster, confident there would be no repeat of the incident.

#

The minkies stopped coming to my surgery soon after that. It bothered me. I walked out into the tall grass one lunch-break and looked for them, but I had to walk a long way before I found any. There was a group of adults, twenty or more, and they weren't gathering seed heads. They were just sitting in smaller groups, blacks and greys together, apparently talking. They looked at me, then went back to their meeting, although two of them stood and tipped their heads back sharply a few times as if they were greeting me.

I don't know if I was surprised when the warning klaxon sounded across at the settlement the next morning. I could hear it in the one-piece shower-toilet, and there were repeaters in every corridor in the base, so everyone knew there was an emergency. I stuck my head out of my cabin, because I hadn't even dressed yet, and there was just the hum of voices where from the civilian support staff in my corridor who had interrupted showers to see what was going on.

I heard someone say that a farmer called Moore had been stabbed to death by minkies while he was in a field, testing the moisture content of an experimental wheat crop. I didn't know him.

"I never thought they'd do that," said my neighbour, Martin Sengupta, who was a hydraulic engineer. "After all these years."

I closed my door and finished dressing.

#

The incident dominated news on the shared message network between colony and base. Some people lived for that network, even though with two thousand colonists and six hundred support we were still at the scale where face-to-face contact was practical. Bob had even painted one entire wall of his cabin with the screen smart-paint so he could download changing landscapes, but I settled for something less intrusive about a meter square.

THEY'VE STILL GOT TROOPS OUT LOOKING FOR THE MINKIES, a colony message said. I asked the screen to scroll down. THEY JUST DISAPPEARED INTO THE WOODS. WE'VE GOT OUR OWN PATROLS. WHY HAVE THEY STARTED DOING THIS AFTER TWENTY-SIX YEARS? Further down, a reply with a base ID said: BECAUSE YOU SHOT ONE OF THEM, ASSHOLE. It reassured me for some reason.

One official message at the end of the thread brought the day's debate to a close. It was from Commander Anne Da Silva, and read: THIS IS A DECLARATION OF MARTIAL LAW. ALL CIVILIAN PATROLS WILL CEASE IMMEDIATELY. PEACEKEEPING TROOPS HAVE BEEN DEPLOYED AND ANY COLONIST FOUND WITH WEAPONS WILL BE DETAINED. ESCORT TROOPS WILL ACCOMPANY ANYONE NEEDING TO WORK IN ISOLATED AREAS BUT ALL OTHER

CIVILIAN PERSONNEL SHOULD REMAIN IN THEIR HOMES UNTIL FURTHER NOTICE.

I had a lot of time for Anne Da Silva.

The next day, despite patrols, an eighteen year old boy was found with spear and club wounds right in the centre of the settlement's neat grid of roads. I had no doubt the minkies were going after the colonists now. There were fewer than 3,000 humans and perhaps millions of minkies, judging by the reports we got from survey teams.

It was a matter of time. They were small, fast and organized, and this was their planet. I thought of going on the network and reminding everyone of the historical parallels, but that would just have made me feel intelligent and wouldn't have altered the situation. I stayed in the base just in case I was wrong and the minkies didn't think of me as one of the good guys.

Bob wasn't in drinking mode that week. He was busy strengthening perimeters and checking security monitoring with his team, puffing and red-faced all the time. He really needed to get his weight down. I ended up in the military bar, a single room with low-alcohol beer in a pay dispenser and cupboard full of those irritating skill games embedded in clear polymer globes. I hated their smug little voices telling me the game was over and that I could try again. Anne Da Silva was sitting at a table on her own, turning one of the games over and over in her hands. She never struck me as the game-playing type.

"How's it going, Commander?"

She looked up at me and patted the cushion on the seat next to her. "Minkies three, colonists nil." She had those bruise-coloured marks under her eyes that people with Indian or Mediterranean blood got when they were very tired. "And we're holding four colonists for carrying offensive weapons."

I sat down. "Knives?"

"Oh no, guns. Didn't you know? They started out with an issue of small calibre rifles for what was euphemistically called agricultural use. Now they've got an arsenal of homemade pieces. That's why ray guns never made it out of the comic books, Dr Drew. You can make a very effective rifle out of next to nothing and it's low tech, easy maintenance. You need a bigger calibre to take out a minkie, though, and they're working on that."

She stared at me for a few seconds and I wasn't sure where to look. "It's Frank," I said. "I take it the mood is getting ugly, then."

"I've got a bigger problem with colonists than I have with minkies, if that's what you mean. That's peacekeeping for you."

"I thought we'd selected colonists for stability."

"We're on the third generation now. They've reverted to being regular humans. Civilized, polite, and always a drink or a grievance away from turning back into savages."

I didn't ask her what she based that view upon because I knew the detail would be depressing. "If there's anything else I can do, ask."

'I'm considering talking directly to the minkies. Want to help? They probably associate you with more positive human attitudes. There's only you, Bryant and Houlihan who seem to give a damn about them."

I was a second rate doctor but I was as good with minkies as anyone. For a moment, I grasped excellence of a kind, and it felt good and warm in my chest. "Of course."

I hadn't seen any minkies for a while now, not even injured ones. It was as if they'd stopped fighting each other.

#

It was the end of the second week since the first stabbing. Troops were searching colonists' homes and confiscating weapons, but there had been no more minkie raids. I walked out into the grassland with Bryant, a system engineer who liked practicing his linguistic skills on minkies, and a discreetly armed Da Silva. Small numbers, low profile, she said. It was the first chilly morning, an early sign of winter approaching.

We were a kilometre out from base before we saw our first minkie.

I had no idea how they worked out whether we were good or bad humans in their books, unless they recognized me or Bryant. I assumed we all looked the same to them. I certainly couldn't tell one minkie from another very easily even now.

This one was grey. It walked up to us with its swaying, side to side gait. It was carrying a spear in its hand rather than in a holder across its back, and there was an intricately woven red strap across its steel-shiny chest fur. Bryant began jerking his head back in that greeting gesture and I followed suit immediately.

Da Silva sat down in a dusty patch of earth in the grass. It struck me as brave, but I had confidence she knew what she was doing. The minkie sat down too and there we all were, sitting in a circle and staring at each other, waiting. They really did remind me of sloths. It was the tapering muzzle as much as the body shape.

Bryant made the grief gesture. His humming wasn't good, but the minkie appeared to get the point, because it began a series of clicks and hisses that it repeated carefully. You got to recognize speech patterns in time. Bryant spent half an hour repeating parts of the sequence until sweat began beading on his bald patch. I tried to help out. Eventually the minkie scraped a humanoid stick figure with its middle finger in the dust in front of Da Silva: an exaggerated long shape, with a massively oversized head. So that was how they saw us.

"They want the kid who killed the minkie," Bryant said. "They know he hasn't been punished. They saw him walking around. If we hand him over they'll leave us alone."

It struck me as a request any nation would make of another. Would we grant it? I looked at Da Silva, but there was nothing, absolutely nothing on her face that I could read. "I'll contact them here this time tomorrow," she said. "Can you explain that, Bryant? I need to think."

We walked back to the base in total silence. I wasn't going to ask her what she was going to do. She was a month away from HQ and ten years from Earth, and none of us had that much time. It was her decision.

She went back to the site with Bryant the next morning, or so he told me. She didn't ask me to go. There was no reason why she should have, but I was hurt just the same.

Bryant said she was handing the kid over to them and that I should prepare for casualties at some point.

#

My personal pager sounded around lunchtime and asked me to stand by. I hit the cascade call-out alarm to alert all paramedic-trained personnel on-base, put my report on save and went down to what was the central assembly point. Troops were taking up positions, and I knew they were bringing in the kid from civilian custody.

Da Silva stopped in her brisk walk past me. "Crank up that infirmary, Frank," she said. "We've had to fire warning shots and there's a transport of colonists four minutes behind us. Plus minkies."

I could have stayed in the infirmary, and I should have. I wasn't a spectator. But I had to watch because I thought something important was going to happen, and I didn't want her to think I was a coward. I followed her outside.

The gates of the newly erected perimeter fence – Bob's latest project – were locked shut. Through them I could see the dust plume from a transport a minute away, and when I looked around I could see five black minkies on the inside of the fence, just standing to one side of the sentry booth. There were probably scores more in the grassland nearby, but I couldn't see any movement: there was just the scent of sulphur.

A dozen soldiers with visors drawn down stood around the gate, and there were others moving around the flat roofs of the base buildings. The colonists' transport pulled up just short of the gates and two men in overalls stepped down, both with rifles. The weapons looked stylishly simple against the attachment-adorned guns the troops carried. They didn't look deadly at all.

"We insist on civilian jurisdiction," said one of the men. "That kid was cleared."

"You were offered the opportunity to hand the detainee over yourself." Da Silva was a meter from the mesh gate, holding her rifle across her body although it was already supported by her webbing. "As military commander, I have the right to invoke martial law if I feel the colony faces serious danger. If I don't resolve this, we'll all be dead within a year. They'll pick us off."

"The minkies are animals. They'll kill him. You should be punishing them, not us."

"If they're animals, they have no responsibility in law for alleged crimes," she said. It was all civilized and rational, except for the guns. "If they're not animals, then they have a right to try someone charged with a crime in their territory. You want to choose?"

The man paused. The rest of the colonists poured out of the transport, thirty or so, and aimed their guns into the compound. Troops raised their rifles around me and it felt as if they had done so all in one tidal movement. The two groups stood, weapons levelled against each other.

"There are two thousand of us. We could take him."

Da Silva hadn't aimed her weapon up to that point, but she levelled it and her body didn't move at all. I didn't know how she could do that so easily. "You take another step and I'll order fire," she said. "Just go back to your homes."

"If you hand that boy over, you've as good as murdered him."

There was a silence, and I could hear the grass rustling. The minkies were watching, but how much of this they could understand I just didn't know. They weren't stupid. They could see the guns, and they knew what guns did.

Then they stood up. There were hundreds of them, blacks and greys, all with spears and clubs and right behind the colonists. The spear-carriers had their weapons poised, a bizarre army of javelin throwers, absolutely still. Lowest tech would beat low tech with those numbers. None of the colonists moved. They didn't even look behind them. But they must have known from the smell and the rustling at their backs that they were cut off.

"No," I shouted. I held my arms up; I had no idea why. The minkies furthest from me turned their heads towards me. It was a stupid thing to do, as stupid as saying no to a dog, but I did it anyway. And it was stupid to shout in a tense situation and risk startling someone into firing.

A couple of colonists risked a glance over their shoulders. Suddenly the rest started to lower their rifles. I saw a flicker of movement to my left, and for a moment I thought one of the soldiers was going to open fire. Trained or not, kids could panic. But they kept their rifles level, and the colonists got into their transport, started the engine and swung round back onto the dirt road.

The whole incident had lasted less than four minutes. The gates opened and minkies streamed in, more than I'd ever seen together at one time. Two military police brought the colonist boy out of a nearby building and the minkies surrounded him like sheepdogs, nudging him out of the gate and onto the road. A two-man transport followed with an armed escort, just in case the colonists had changed their minds down the road, and kicked up a cloud of khaki dust that gradually hid the minkies from view. All I could see was the vehicle and the boy, short and shaven-headed and altogether too nondescript to be the pivot of a diplomatic drama.

I didn't watch the procession any further. Da Silva caught my eye.

"Brave choice," I said.

"The only one I had." There was a sweat mark down the back of her shirt even though it was a cool day.

"Do you want to talk about it?"

"No. My decision. No point burdening you."

"Do we know why the kid did it?"

Da Silva nodded. "He wanted to hunt."

She walked back into the main building, and never mentioned my stupid display. I went back to the infirmary. It was a full day before the shock of the incident hit me. I found it hard to sleep that night because I kept thinking how easily I could have started the whole crowd firing.

I passed my sleepless hours wondering what Anne Da Silva did for fun. Perhaps she didn't have any: she was isolated by rank among her own, and by age among the civilian workforce.

On the other hand, a doctor – even a colonial quack like me – had something of a neutral position. I practiced asking her to go for a beer until eventually I fell asleep.

#

The following days were silent rather than quiet. Troops still patrolled the settlement and confiscated arms, although some of the colonists had shown up at the base to surrender guns and ammunition. I was still on stand-by. I was walking across to the canteen when I ran into Bob and he told me that the colonist boy had been dumped back at the settlement, bruised and torn but alive. I thought I should drop by Da Silva's office.

I didn't fully expect to find her there, but she was sitting at her desk in the usual way. She looked tired, and I avoided staring too hard in case she had been crying. I don't know why I expected to see that. I just did, and I didn't want to embarrass her by noticing.

"So he's alive," I said.

"Seems so."

"Any idea what happened?"

"Bryant said the kid had to gather food for the family he's left without a provider. He has to do it every week as a condition of staying alive."

"Surprised?"

"You could say that." She paused. "Bryant says they

wanted to show us how civilized they were. Maybe you could find out next time a minkie comes in for treatment. They seem to like you."

#

I didn't see another minkie that month. In fact, only six came in the next twelve weeks, all greys with minor injuries that looked accidental. There were no battle wounds. I cleaned them up and waved goodbye.

There was a woven basket left at my door one morning, red and black, like the spear strap we'd seen on one of the minkies that autumn. They'd never done that before. After that I saw them when I went walking, and we would stop and converse as best we could, but they didn't come for treatment. The basket was a farewell.

One of them told me they were "waiting to watch the invaders." I didn't fully understand.

They seemed to have stopped their wars for the time being. Perhaps we were the common enemy now, and when they were done with us they would resume their food disputes as if we had never been there. Da Silva was right. There were millions of them and a few thousand of us. If they ever chose to oust us, the numbers were on their side.

#

These days I still drink occasionally with Bob, but I spend my time with Anne Da Silva. She makes a fine Goan curry because that's where her family came from, so I do have a little of colonial India around to remind me how things can turn out for the conqueror in the long run. Anne persuaded me to contact Earth to confirm if my mother is now dead. She thinks I need closure.

Sometimes I visit the minkie encampments in the woodland five kilometres from base, and I'm learning much more about their physiology and diseases. I take it carefully.

One day being the kind doctor may no longer be enough to save me. One thing's certain: I can truthfully say I'm the best minkie doctor around.

And I've decided to erase the Earth-time clock from my organizer tonight. My bank manager can send me statements when he pleases.

There's no hurry. This is my orient. I suit it down to the ground.

DEATH, TAXES, AND MACKEREL

(First published in *On Spec*, Spring 2002. Written as an exercise at Clarion East Workshop, 2000.)

Death wasn't all it was cracked up to be for Julia.

The first thing she saw when she opened her eyes was an unimaginative bouquet on the table at her hospital bedside. Yellow chrysanthemums: God, she really hated chrysanthemums and their musty wet scent. She made a grab for the small card propped against the vase, and missed. A nurse rushed in to her field of vision.

"The card," Julia said, still hoarse from revival. Chrysanthemums had been banned from the house when she was a girl: her mother claimed they were bad luck, funeral flowers. "Who sent that?"

"The International Revenue, ma'am," said the nurse. "Shall I read the card? It says, *nice try, welcome back, love from all at District 6A, Appeal Court ruled you were temporarily non-resident, not dead.*"

"Bastards," said Julia.

#

Julia Sinstadt had proved death was avoidable but she was still struggling a little with the taxes. Her fight with taxation was the last frontier in a long life built on winning battles. She won at business and she won in the divorce courts and she won on property deals, and she went on winning until the winning was all that she had left. She was 120. She wanted to win the last game of all.

"You have to view it like joy-riding," said the taxation lawyer. He was Hatton or King: she had trouble caring which of the firm's partners he was. She settled on Hatton. "For example, taking a car isn't the same as stealing it. In law, the prosecution has to prove you intended to permanently deprive the owner of their vehicle, or you're just a joy-rider. So if you want to take advantage of the tax benefits in death, you can't intend to resurrect yourself. You have to mean to be really, really dead. That's the legal argument they used on appeal."

"Then," said Julia Sinstadt, "find another way to get round the International Revenue." She smoothed her well-kept hands down her well-cut suit. Age didn't excuse a sloppy appearance: she was sharp and chic. "I will *not* have my money go to the government. I'll decide where it's spent – every last penny."

Cryo-suspension had been her accountant's idea. Die intestate by your own hand, chill down for four months, then come back to life before the deadline and claim the estate before it went to the government. Only beneficiaries had to pay inheritance tax. You couldn't inherit from yourself, so you didn't pay a penny. It was a test case.

And, medically, Julia really had been dead: no cardiac, respiratory or higher brain activity had been detectable. But she hadn't been dead enough for the taxman.

"They did allow you a small rebate, though," said Hatton.

They were getting sharp, the International Revenue. But she would be sharper.

#

Hatton had a assembled a retinue of scientists and technicians, each with a novel idea to get round a stranglehold-tight universal tax system on Julia's behalf. Their ingenuity bordered on the fantastic.

"If you're prepared to risk it, we can get you off the planet, whiz you a few light years away at 90 per cent of light speed and bring you back," he said, performing rough calculations as he talked. "Time dilation means you'll be a year older but a hundred years will have passed on Earth, you can qualify for full non-residency, your investments will have grown fantastically, and – "

Julia fixed him with an unemotional eye. "Financial regulations night be even harsher next century. My stock might have plummeted. And besides, you won't be around for me to sue the pants off you if anything goes wrong."

"Okay." He tapped up another bright idea from the inlaid surface of his desk. "There's this chap who has a genetically-enhanced dolphin. It's currently bringing a test case in the courts to prove it's smart enough to be classed as a minor in law."

He switched the video playback from his desk-top onto the display wall, where a sleek and shiny bottle-nose suddenly arched out of a pool. A technician held out an extra-large keypad and the dolphin tapped diligently with its beak. I'M AS SMART AS YOU, CHIMP-FACE, flashed up on a panel, one letter at a time.

Hatton beamed. "If the dolphin's action is successful, you can give it your fortune on paper and then it can give you it all back as a gift. Gifts from minors don't attract tax."

"What if it's smart enough to keep it all?" Julia asked.

"What's it going to spend it on, mackerel?"

"Not being able to *spend* it all doesn't mean you don't *want* it all." She leaned forward, her suspicion honed by years of wrangling with the legal profession. "And is it a client of yours, by the way?"

He froze for just the merest split of a second.

"Yes," he said. "There's nothing in the bar association rules precluding it – "

"Next," Julia said.

The ideas went on. They were mostly crazy or dangerous or both. Julia found she had started to chip away the real platinum polish on her manicured thumb-nail in frustration.

"Is that the best you can do for the retainer I pay you?" she asked.

"Well, there's always cloning," said the lawyer. "I know it takes a few years to grow an adult body – and it's only legal in Paraguay – but it's worth a look."

Julia was nothing if not thorough. She hadn't made billions by ignoring possibilities. She had imagined a few brief years on her retirement atoll savouring her greatest defeat of authority before finally accepting the time's impersonal victory over her. Cheating death on a grander scale had not been part of the plan. It intrigued her. "Go on."

"We create a clone from you and you give her – yourself – your cash as a gift. Provided we do it a year before you die, no gift or inheritance tax is payable. The clone needs to have only a few genetic differences from your own genome to make her a separate person in law. If it's a straight cloning job, you're back with the problem of not really being seriously dead, you see."

Julia had died before. She had faced that moment when she pressed the button to administer the drugs and the bright beam of light drew her in. She knew what lay on at least one of its many sides. And, at 120, she was a little less afraid of it than she had imagined she could be. Death for her was now an administrative detail like registering patents.

"I'll take it," she said. "Can I be a blonde this time round?"

#

The technicians and geneticists, who didn't come any cheaper than the lawyers, explained to her how the process was almost foolproof. They spoke to her of accelerated growth and memory transfers and other ways to create a new Julia Sinstadt. They also told her they put her current life expectancy at two years. It was a good and wise time to start cloning.

Just to ensure the law didn't get too picky, they gave Julia II an assortment of distinctive but trivial single-gene variations, including the ability to curl her tongue lengthways – as well as blonde hair.

"And narrower hips," said Julia the Original. "If we're going to make me different, let's do it right."

"I can't see how that'll do any harm," said the geneticist. "We don't always know how altering some clusters of genes will affect others, but if you don't like the result we can always wipe the board clean and start again, if you know what I mean. Before the memory transfer."

"Will I have to go through childhood again?"

"No, we skip that."

"And I can stay sedated so I don't have to meet me, can't I? I don't think I could cope with that."

"You can afford to have anything you want done, Ms Sinstadt."

"Then take it away, professor," said Julia, and laughed.

They promised her that she wouldn't dream during the process. But somewhere in the not-quite-waking stages, she – or one of her, she thought – began seeing dolphins.

#

Julia II grew rapidly into blonde and perfect health inside four years, and inherited a hundred billion and a lifetime of second-hand memories. She didn't go to see herself held on life support, and she didn't attend her own funeral. She had been 123 when the nursing home finally ended life support and now she was more or less 35. She had liked being 35 before.

One trait that had survived intact was a briskly competitive attitude towards the International Revenue: theirs didn't seem to have diminished with time either. This time they were challenging the use of non-medical cloning with prior intent to avoid lawful taxation.

It was worth their while: she was big revenue to them if they could pin her down. They were not about to give up. And neither was she.

She hired more of the brightest and most bloody-minded lawyers to support Hatton, who was not getting any younger. It was the sort of battle which normally got her adrenaline pumping and swept everything else from the table.

But not this time.

Things felt somehow different, like tasting a favourite childhood treat in later life and wondering what had happened to the flavour. She took a soul-searching trip to Tibet and came back laden with souvenir prayer-flags and model temples.

"For you," she said, and dumped a carrier bag marked I LOVE LHASA on Hatton's desk. "That's the first holiday I've had in twenty years in either body. God, it's so touristy there now. Have you been?"

He appeared to duck the question. "You've changed, Ms Sinstadt."

"Yes, I'm a blonde. I'm supposed to have more fun." She considered the recurring dreams of a frustrated intellectual dolphin, and the nagging urge to give money away to good causes. "I'm getting generous to charity even without the tax breaks. Do you think it's something to do with the cloning?"

#

The geneticist showed Julia the results of test after test. "You're not sick, Ms Sinstadt."

"I didn't think I was. I just wondered how much I changed in the process."

"Well, some altruistic behaviour in organisms is related to distinct genes, just as some genes predispose to violence. But we did warn you we couldn't predict the expression of every single gene before you signed the waiver. It's not like you grew an extra leg or anything."

"No, you're right," she said, and was amazed she felt no hunger for litigation. "Do you think we could patent that gene cluster and sell it to law enforcement agencies?"

"Somebody already has," he said. "And as soon as we settle the legal arguments against using it, I'm sure it'll be a boon to mankind."

That night, she dreamed of the dolphin again. He was a highly intrusive dolphin considering she had only seen him once in a video.

#

Hatton pointed out to her at their monthly conference that she had given away more to good causes that month than she would have paid in tax.

"I know," Julia II said. "I can't help it. It just seemed so – necessary. Look, what happened to that dolphin you represented? The one with the status case?"

"Why do you ask?"

"I keep dreaming about the damn thing. And I never even saw him. Is he still around? It's just something I want to explore. Indulge me."

"I'll get my secretary to look him up," said Hatton.

She dreamed of the dolphin again that night. Usually he appeared in inappropriate places in her dreams: she would be standing in her office, and turn to see her carpet rippling like water and the dolphin rising from it in an arc of foam. He would emerge from cupboards, from parted grass, from between curtains. He seemed to spend a lot of time out of water. He broke all the dolphin rules. He was not the cute, squeaking friend of mankind: he was a wild dolphin, smart and savage, fighting in gangs and brokering alliances.

When she woke, the dream was still vivid. She wrote it down and saved the details for later study. What was she telling herself? She pondered and wondered for a few days, and then gave up and rang a therapist.

"The dolphin is your creative side," said the therapist, at $1,000 a half hour. "He is telling you that you can solve your conflicts through unconventional routes. He is telling you that you that you must use your inner dolphin."

"Really?" she said, and although $1,000 was small change to her she made a note to cancel the fool's contract. Her limo took her back to her office and as she watched the silenced press of people she swept past, a thought struck her.

It wasn't the inner dolphin who would give her a creative solution to her feud with the taxman. It was the outer one. The *real* one.

#

Julia II sat drinking juice at an open-air bar in a seaside resort watching kids frolicking in the shallows. In the mid-distance, she saw a fin slicing through the water and for an instant she pictured screaming carnage. But it was just a dolphin. She watched it swim up to the small pier nearby. It whacked a bell with its beak and brought the bar owner running with a bucket of mackerel.

"Go on, get out," he yelled. "That's the fifth bucket today. No show, no tips, okay?" As he passed Julia, he paused, looking a little embarrassed. "I know he's cute, but he's really unreliable. Doesn't always show up, you know? He used to do quizzes."

"Quizzes?"

"He spells on that big keyboard thing over there."

At the end of the owner's pointing arm was indeed an oversize keyboard, lashed to one leg of the pier. Julia followed the rest of the gesture to a display board, encrusted with seagull droppings. "Thanks," she said. "Can I call him?"

"Sure. Here, you might need this keypad for him to

understand some of the complex stuff. Make sure you've got a mackerel with you. He don't do nothin' without gettin' paid."

Julia sat on the edge of the pier and cupped her hands around her mouth. "Hey! Over here!" The sea broke and foamed and a blue-grey polished dome rose from it in an arc that jogged something way back in a memory. She had a sudden and overwhelming urge to donate all her money to charity.

"It's you," she said to the dolphin. "The enhanced dolphin. The court case. Archie?"

The dolphin flipped to the oversize keyboard and tapped furiously.

DAMN USELESS SHYSTERS

"Yes, he's my lawyer too," she said. "But you won the case."

YES BUT NO MORE FREE FISH. THEY CAN'T KEEP A SENTIENT BEING IN CAPTIVITY. GOTTA WORK.

"The price of freedom, eh?"

I PREFER MACKEREL. LOOKING FOR AN ACCOUNTANT? I'M GOOD WITH FIGURES.

"Maybe not, but I might have an attractive offer for you. How would you like to head up an educational foundation for non-human citizens?"

WHAT'S IN IT FOR ME?

"Mackerel, a secure home, that sort of thing."

AND YOU?

"Winning. I want to win."

LET'S TALK, said Archie, in a shimmering sequence of LEDs. WHO ARE WE FIGHTING?

"Do you feel oppressed? Do you think you're being discriminated against because you're of cetacean extraction?"

THEY NEVER LET YOU FORGET IT.

"And you would like the barriers that prevent you from achieving your full potential to be removed?"

I HAVE A RIGHT TO MY CULTURAL DIVERSITY.

IS THAT A MACKEREL YOU HAVE THERE?

"Indeed it is, Archie," she said, and lobbed it towards him. "I think we have the makings of a deal."

#

The best thing about non-criminal court actions was that you could conduct them by video-link. Julia was happy. She had no money to her name, on paper at least, and she felt good. She was at her financial adviser's side, by the pool with a pile of shrimp, and watching the proceedings.

The International Revenue's counsel was on his feet a hundred kilometres away and wearing the expression of a man who was losing his case and didn't think it was fair.

"I submit, your honour, that the status of the director of a company is irrelevant," said counsel. "It's the organization which is liable. The director has a duty in law to accept the prevailing customs of the business world and pay his taxes in the appropriate manner."

The image split. Counsel for the Cetacean Advancement Foundation stood up in another remote office.

"Your honour, insisting on payment in the human fashion offends my client's cultural and ethnic values. But he is more than willing to pay." Julia thought the lawyer was laying the equality stuff on a tad too thickly. "My client – Mr Bottlenose, as he prefers to be called – has achieved accountancy success through his own efforts and the generous support of the Foundation, which I would remind you is the recipient of Julia Sinstadt II's entire fortune. He wishes to make the tax payment and claim the reduced rate for educational organizations."

"Oh well, if payment has been offered, then I find for the defendant," the judge said. "Mr Bottlenose may make arrangements to pay sums due to the International Revenue in a manner appropriate to his, er, ethnicity."

"We intend to appeal," said the International Revenue's counsel.

The judge was halfway out of his seat and looked irked to be interrupted in mid-flight. "I wouldn't be minded to grant leave for further appeal unless there's new evidence. You might want to think about that before filing those papers." The judge pressed the button on his console and the judgement was downloaded simultaneously to all parties. "Court is now dismissed."

Poolside, Julia applauded and Archie Bottlenose executed a series of triumphant leaps from the water, chittering wildly.

WAY TO GO he typed.

She switched off the video link. "So how do you want to pay?" she asked him.

MACKEREL. A NICE BIG PILE OF MACKEREL. HAVE IT DELIVERED TO THEIR OFFICE.

"That's my boy," Julia II beamed, and lobbed a cupful of shrimp into the pool.

#

After the elation of the mackerel ruling, Julia experienced a sense of disappointing peace: all her giants were slain. She stood on the white sand of her atoll and stared out into the hard bright turquoise horizon, longing for the boardroom.

"Now I'm really dead," she said aloud.

And she was. Without her company and her battles, she might as well have traded places with her decomposed self. Her goal had been the journey. The destination was a pretty dull place to spend another seventy years.

Archie, busy with accounts, was in his office pool, tapping at his oversize calculator. Julia sat down on the mosaic edge and dangled her feet in the water.

BE BORED SOMEWHERE ELSE, DOLL.

"Sorry, Archie. Is it that obvious?"

YOU RUST QUICKER THAN YOU WEAR OUT. GOTTA STAY BUSY.

The empty day stretched before her. She could hear the *fut-fut-fut* of a small boat in the distance, reminding her that everyone but her had a job to do. "Maybe I could start over," she said.

YEAH. GREAT IDEA. NOW I'VE LOST MY PLACE AND I'VE GOT TO START THIS AGAIN.

She took the hint. She walked back down the beach to the jetty. The tang of the sea was a little tangier then, and she thought for a moment that the tide was a long way out: but no, she was on the atoll, and the tide didn't drop that far. She sniffed the air and walked on.

Fut-fut-fut. It was louder now.

The small boat chugged past the end of the jetty and swung round to tie up. She thought it was supplies. She ran to the end of the planking and stared down at the boat, which was towing a smaller tender.

It stank to high heaven and beyond. She stared at the pile of ripe mackerel. The skipper – a frowning man with a handkerchief knotted over his nose and mouth – silently handed her a delivery note, swung a line onto the pier, secured the tender and then cast off again even before she had opened the envelope.

It was from the International Revenue. The note said they were pleased to be able to forward Mr A. Bottlenose's rebate for the previous tax year.

Julia stared at the pile of rotting fish and felt her throat tighten. Her mouth began to fill with unwanted saliva. She was angry and upset and close to vomiting.

But slowly, very slowly, a grin made its way across her face.

Now she had something to live for again.

EVIDENCE

(Guilty admission: I have no idea where this was published, but the manuscript dates from 1998. Reynolds was originally going to feature in my Wess'har novels, but in the end I swapped him for a female cop called Shan Frankland, and... well you know the rest.)

There were at least a dozen bodies in the pit as far as the subsoil scan could detect.

The screen showed them aligned in an orderly way, neat-piled like logs. Just one spoiled the arrangement, lying at right angles across the mass, two limbs twisted at angles, the other six folded along the sides of the body.

Reynolds turned away from the display. He could see the top layer of corpses for himself: the sandy soil had been disturbed and the chitin beneath was still as bright as glass. It was the last thing he needed right then, with just a week left of this tour of duty. He would never sort out the paperwork in that time. He didn't like handing cases on to the Relief. So he was going home late after all, just when time was what he didn't have to spare.

They were little bodies, not much more than a meter long. For all the gravity of the situation he couldn't stop them reminding him of expensive chocolates moulded into spiral shells, glossy, marbled in earth colours. He'd bought a box for Jenny, a compensation for all the morning sickness she was suffering at the time he left for this duty.

"We called you as soon as we found it," the foreman said. Reynolds concentrated on the man's faceplate, although he was peripherally aware of the rest of the survey gang grouped out of focus behind their boss. "We need to get it sorted as soon as possible." There was a pause. "Please."

"You know the rules," Reynolds said. "Same as on Earth. We find remains, we assume it's a crime scene until we have evidence to show otherwise. However old it looks, however weird it looks. You can't assume anything, chum – I've known a man dump his wife in a peat bog to make her look like a thousand-year-old burial." These were the first relatively intact bodies he'd seen on the planet, although there were plenty of charred, smashed husks in the ruined settlements. "We've got remains of buildings all round here and signs of an organised burial. And I don't *care* if they look like bloody lobsters, we still do it by the book. Full investigation procedure."

"But this is *another planet*. They're aliens. Even if this *was* a murder, what the hell has it got to do with us now?"

"You got a different book of regulations for this place? Subsection five, how to deal with alien cadavers?"

"No."

"Then we follow the procedures we've got."

The foreman threw his hands up, and the reflection off his faceplate masked any expression of anger. Lost time equalled lost bonuses: it was remarkably law-abiding of the man even to report the find to Enforcement with that pressure on him. Reynolds could sympathise with impatience right then.

"Have you touched anything?" *Please don't let it be a crime, anything out of the ordinary, I need to be home fast, Jen's going into labour in two weeks.* "I need to know."

"Just the damage the excavator did. And I scraped back some of the sand to see what we'd hit."

"No souvenirs?" Survey teams could never be trusted to

leave artefacts alone. Petty pilfering – company property, archaeological material, whatever wasn't bolted to the planet - made up most of his law enforcement workload. "They're a nice little earner, aren't they?"

The foreman held out a transparent sample bag in clumsy gloved fingers. It contained a small thickened disc: Reynolds' immediate thought was *powder compact*. It looked like the antique one Jenny treasured, but could never find the powder to fill, right down to the inscribed designs on the case. He resisted the urge to take it out of the bag and prise it open.

"Just that," said the foreman. "It was right on the top layer."

"Thank you."

"So it was a murder, right?"

"And what makes you think that?" Reynolds turned the compact over and over in his hand, struck by the intricacy of the engraving. "We might need an archaeologist here, not a detective."

The foreman's face betrayed a slight smugness. He beckoned Reynolds over to the far side of the pit, and brushed back the sand which had trickled back over the bodies. They knelt down on all fours, and the man's finger traced a small circle on what looked like a shiny shell of a skull.

"I don't know much about forensics, but I know a puncture hole in a crab shell, and that looks damn like one to me," the foreman said. "The poor little sod was hit. Hard." He reached further in and touched the end of a sliver of some stiff, dark substance, waggling it about: Reynolds decided it was a tool of some sort. "With this, I expect. But like I said - not our planet, nobody left alive, so why are we bothering with all this?"

Reynolds felt his heart sink. He now had cause - whether he liked it or not - to treat this as an unnatural death investigation. The grave could have been months or centuries old: the whole area – the whole planet, it seemed – had been scorched clean by fire, the end results of sporadic flares from the planet's sun. But the regulations were clear. He followed regulations.

"Sod it," he said to himself.

"You going to cordon it off, then?"

"Yes, I'm going to cordon it off." Resigned, he summoned the bot, and it detached itself from his vehicle and trundled towards him. "I'd be prepared to be off this site for some days if I were you."

Reynolds waited until the entire survey team had loaded back into their wagon before beginning the bot's program. "Layer scan down to ten meters," he said. "Record locations for imaging. Start an object scan at two meters from victims."

Victims.

He'd admitted it to himself now. He wandered back to the vehicle and caught up on his lunch while the bot swept and recorded. He peered at the compact thing through the plastic, trying to smooth the bag down with one thumb while his other hand was busy with a sandwich. Powder compacts and chocolates: God, he needed a break badly if all he saw in this sterile ochre wasteland were the fripperies of human luxury. But it was a pretty thing, that disc, pleasingly made, metallic, weighty in the palm. It would have been a nice find for an archaeologist.

He squeezed it, and thought he could hear faint, irregular crackling sounds, but they stopped.

Whatever the object turned out to be, it was now evidence.

#

Fifth day, Late Harvest.

I refuse to die forever.

I explained it to Muzi and even she thought I was insane, but I believe she sees the proof now. The dormancy is possible. I proved it. And when the rivers boil dry and the buildings of generations crumble in the heat, we — or rather our unborn — will survive.

I thought I would find more sisters willing to risk the dormancy with me, but it's difficult. The ones we need most – the scholars, constructors, thinkers – prefer to spend their time finding repositories for our archives, preserving them simply to prove we were once here. I don't call that surviving.

Dormancy is our only hope. I've checked the tank of clickers again. There are definite signs of hatching, and those creatures have been heated and desiccated for a year or more. It will work for us, too. We're still not so very different, for all our evolution and advanced ways.

I'm feeling very tired now. I'll record more tomorrow.

#

Good old decomposing bodies. That was what he needed. Reynolds knew where he was with human flesh in all its stages, whether laid low by violence, or mangled in an accident, or just at the end of its allotted span. He had a feel for it. But it was hard to know where to start with things in shells.

He sat down cross-legged in the sand, no easy feat in an environment suit. Maybe, if he saw the scene from the aliens' eye-level, he'd get a feel for the sequence of events. This world had not always been dead.

From where he sat, the smashed hemispheres of child-scale buildings made a skyline of broken eggshells, punctuated by stumps of what once might have been bushes. He tried to picture the little lobster-cricket things in life: fast moving, busy, twitchy. Milling. No, terrestrial insects milled. These had intelligent purpose. They built structures and created objects.

He tried again. Yellowing sky, like snow was coming: no, it never snowed here, and anyway that was pre-catastrophe, and it would have been bright and sunny. A disaster looming coming: what would his own kind have done? Panic, looting, violence, the mindless rush from here to nowhere in particular, just *away*.

It fell into place. He superimposed a township on the

burned landscape, and groups of the creatures in conflict, and one small band being herded towards a mass grave to their deaths because they were somehow the wrong sort, the wrong tribe, the wrong whatever.

"We're not the only ones, then," he said aloud. The bot paused in its drilling and scanning.

"Instruction?" it asked.

"Ignore that," Reynolds said. "I was just saying that humans aren't the only creature which turn on themselves in a crisis."

He knew it meant nothing to the bot. It resumed its work. It was a surveying tool, not an AI or anything remotely companionable. Grain by grain, layer by layer, it was recording the sonar image of the pit and drilling out soil samples.

Whoever killed the crickets was probably long dead, Reynolds decided. All he needed was confirmation of the timing of the last solar flares from someone in Astrophys, something tangible to reassure him that there could be nobody left to bring to justice. He might even be able to wrap up the investigation inside ten days, and make it home before the baby arrived. Things were looking up after all.

He scrambled upright, cursing the ache in his knees and ankles, and headed back to the transport.

A message was waiting for him. It was a response to his request for assistance. An archaeologist on the way from base, four days away, and the last flare had been a century ago. He could file the incident under history now. It was clear no criminal investigation was expected.

In the meantime, all he could do was think and work his way through the field rations.

He took the compact out of his inside pocket and turned it over and over in his hands. Just a grim piece of another world's history. But it was a very pretty piece, clearly treasured enough for a cricket-thing to clutch in its final moments. A cricket-thing with fears and maybe family, like him.

Almost human, Reynolds thought, and pocketed it. He could swear it had crackled again.

#

They're panicking now. All my neighbours have gone with their broods: where they think they'll find refuge I have no idea. We can't outrun the firestorms when they come. Even Muzi shows signs of losing her nerve. She keeps asking me if it's going to work. All I can do is tell her that it worked for the clickers, and we're not that different from them physiologically.

We will shrivel and dry into paper, but our unborn will survive, dormant, until the temperature and humidity are at the right level to support life again. How many times has this place been ravaged by the fires? We know of at least a dozen from the soil records. Each time life returns. We have to hold on to the evidence and trust our natural defence mechanisms.

I have an unborn brood now. They'll have all my skills and knowledge, of course, but they won't know what it was truly like to live through all this. I'm not sure if our fragile cities will survive the fire: I don't know if our young be able to find the archives we'll leave for them. And they'll know little of me, beyond the fact that my corpse was there to protect them. So I've recorded all this, all the small detail, so they'll know who and what I was, and how many dreams I had for them. When will they finally end the dormancy and begin life? I have no way of knowing whether it will be seasons or aeons.

It's very hard to carry unborn and know you will never see them.

#

The screen's image of the pit and its contents was composed of pinpricks of colour. It lit their faces: Reynolds glanced at the archaeologist, fresh from base, and decided it wasn't a flattering light for a woman at all.

"Look," she said. "I think we have a clear pattern here." She ran her little finger along the lines of acid green. "The soil's been stained, probably with body fluids, and then these scuff marks in the different layers – I'd say they were killed a little way from the edge of the pit and dragged to it and pushed in. I don't know enough about these things to say if this is a normal posture, with the forelegs drawn up, or whether that's a reflex. Death throes. Damn sure they didn't pop in for a snooze and just nod off, though."

Reynolds could see it now. It was like someone pointing out figures in a cloudscape. One minute it was a mess of random shapes, the next it was a picture. He rotated the three–D through 90 degrees. He liked it better when he couldn't make it out. Now he couldn't stop himself seeing images of panic and shattering chitin, and it surprised him, because he had long since learned to shut all that out and deal only in hard evidence. He really did need that break.

He made a conscious effort to breathe steadily. "Would you look at the bodies, Ms Collier?" he asked. "I've got them bagged now. I'd just like a second opinion on the likely causes of death."

She nodded, and began easing her gloves back on. Not that he'd needed to refrigerate the corpses. They were mummified, dry-roasted: they weren't decomposing any time soon. But it seemed irreverent to leave them out in the open like stacked logs.

"What do you reckon?" Collier asked.

"Blows to what looks like the head," Reynolds said. He pulled the thin fabric back from one of the creatures. "It's a bit of a bugger, trying to identify something when you're not even sure what body part you're looking at. But I decided this looked like a logical place for a brain, if you're built like a cricket or a prawn."

"Not bad," said Collier. "Good guess. Not that I've seen these before, either. If we assume they died at the time of the last major solar flares in this system, they've been dead at least a hundred years in our terms." She gave him an odd little smile. "You like to do things by the book, don't you?"

"That's what the book's there for. To deal with the unknown."

They stared at the little corpse on the makeshift slab: tiny, fragile, finely hinged and articulated like a complex clockwork toy. Reynolds fancied he could see a large-eyed face in the swirled tortoise-shell browns and ambers.

Chocolates, he thought. *Powder compact.*

"I'd say a couple of blows to the carapace with that instrument you found," Collier said. She indicated the fracture lines with that little finger nail again. "Look, this one first – then this blow. The second fracture runs into the first one and stops. That's how you can tell the sequence of blows. Not that it matters now, I suppose."

"They're all like that, bar one," Reynolds said. "One had no signs of trauma at all. The one lying on the top."

Collier did a side to side nod of her head, as if weighing up the probabilities.

"Well, I'd say she was the last one in."

"She?"

"She. Eggs. At least I'm pretty sure they're eggs. You weren't far out with that prawn analogy. They were all pregnant. That might not be significant. Then again, it might be the motive."

Pregnant? Pregnant females slaughtered. One of the classic excesses of war, the ultimate destruction, and Reynolds had always wanted to think only the sickest of sick humanity did that. He tried not to look too shaken. He'd vomited at a post mortem during his police cadet days, and never lived it down. But this was getting too close to his own preoccupations. He thought of Jenny, pregnant and managing all alone while he was out here, and the guilt crushed him for a moment.

"I don't suppose the eggs could still be viable."

Collier shrugged. "I'm not a biologist."

"Just asking."

"Are you okay?"

"Go on. So she's last in."

"So she was either forced to kill the others and pushed in, cause of death unknown as yet, or the perpetrators changed their method for some reason."

Reynolds found himself juggling the little metal compact in his pocket. It crackled and ticked briefly. He didn't want to reveal it to the archaeologist: somehow he had imagined he would open it, although he knew he had neither the skills nor experience to interpret its use. He turned it over and over in his palm, and felt the engravings through the thin protective film that still covered it. It had meant something to one of these little creatures, to take it to her death. He didn't want to surrender it.

"This is evidence," he said at last. He took the compact out of his coverall and held it out to her. "What do you reckon it is?"

She held it near the light. "Pretty," she said. "And fascinating. But no idea, I'm afraid. Could I take it to –"

"I'm sure we'll release it for research at some time," Reynolds said. "We won't be using it at any trial."

He held out his hand for her to return the treasure. When he slipped it back inside his jacket, it *tick-tick-ticked* again. He wondered if he could get one of the chemists at base to make up some old-style face powder for Jen.

#

The medics say the quickest way to die, and the safest for the unborn, is a blow to the central nervous system. I am the strongest: these are my friends and respected colleagues. So I'll do what's necessary. I caught Muzi whining in her cell last night, and she tried to hide it from me, but I knew she was frightened. I told her it wouldn't hurt. I wouldn't let her suffer.

She said she was afraid of not knowing what her unborn would eventually wake to. There was nothing I could do to reassure her, but I let her have my recorder for a while so she could store a message to her future children. That machine has been a huge comfort to me. I keep it with me at all times now, just in case the fires come earlier than predicted and we don't make it to the site.

I don't suppose it matters where our bodies wait out the storm. But we thought a pit might offer better protection from crushing and other damage. Our unborn can lie dormant through heat and desiccation, but if they're crushed, they will never hatch.

I have the pick now. I've practised a little, swinging cleanly, trying to get one good deep blow without flinching. I'll have to do this a dozen times, and I'm so afraid I won't make a clean job of it.

We dug the pit yesterday. Enough sand so that when we roll the bodies in, they will land gently. Then it will be my turn, and I will cover my sisters, and burrow down beneath to lie with them.

There'll be nobody to speed me on my way. I think that frightens me a little.

#

"So we ship them back."

"Yeah."

"I'm done here, then."

"Outside your jurisdiction, I'd say. By quite a few decades."

Reynolds and Collier edged around each other in the transport, both trying to get out of their environment suits without colliding with the other. The air was stale with the smell of dry-ration lasagne and sweat. *Home in five days, only two days late, Jen.* He thought of chocolates and the crush of people back home, of stepping out of this wasteland and hanging it up in the locker like his envo suit, a thing done with. Beings had been killed and there was nothing he could have done, nor anything he could do about it now. It should have made it easier. It didn't.

He pulled the tabs on the packs of reconstituted lasagne and let them heat up and swell. The meal didn't go down easily, and he stared down at the uniform-sized lumps spread with precision over the stark white sheets of pasta. All flesh made him queasy now.

"Coffee?" Collier said.

"No thanks."

"I thought all cops were hard cases."

"I don't know – I suppose it's the fact they were females and they had eggs and there were personal possessions there. Even if they were alien."

"I can see this has upset you," she said.

"Not upset."

"Because they were females?"

"Because someone got away with killing them." He didn't know the answer was even there until it spilled out. "I know it's irrelevant, but it's eating at me."

"Well, I think you can assume the killer died a pretty unpleasant death too. Nobody got out of this alive." Collier struck him as a cold common sense sort of woman, and he was inclined to listen to her. "No family left to grieve. No risk of the killer enjoying a long and prosperous life, or repeating the crime. It's closed. Walk away from it."

"I will," he said, and suddenly became aware of the little compact thing pressed into his flesh through his pocket. It ticked sporadically. Perhaps there was something broken inside. "I just don't like loose ends, that's all."

#

We finally had to leave the colony. Panic does terrible things to reasonable minds. Our neighbours said we were sick and perverted to be deliberately carrying young when the storms came. They said we should do the decent thing and destroy our eggs like the others had done. I tried to explain that they would survive, but the smoke was already visible on the horizon, and no amount of rational explanation could prevail in the face of that.

I'm the last left alive now, and this is my final entry. I wasn't sure if I could do it. But when I saw my sisters' fear at the encroaching smoke, it suddenly became clear and easy. My practice paid off. And they became calm, too: right up to the last, Muzi helped me lay them down in the pit until her turn came.

I don't want to dwell on that. Her offspring will understand the need.

Looking back, it saddens me that nearly all my kind accepted the inevitability of extinction. In a way, we nearly killed ourselves off: we didn't trust the evidence of our own history. Apart from our group, I don't believe there are any others waiting for the dormancy.

But we can rebuild. We'll live again through our young, and those young will be challengers, imbued with our enquiring spirit, less traditional than our generation, and the mothers of those who will be even better placed to survive when the next fires come. They may even find a way to avoid the dormancy altogether.

It's odd to think we'll be here for so many cycles before the rains come again and life starts over. If there were creatures from other worlds who might come and find us, what would they think?

I can see the flame front now. It's time to burrow down alongside my sisters, and that's unpleasant, but it won't be for long. Not now. If the sand does not take me, the heat will.

I should stop recording now. Look at those patterns in the sky. It's really quite beautiful. Goodbye, children. All you have to do is wait.

#

The mining team had already moved back in by the time the freighter arrived. Reynolds could see no reason to delay their operation any further. Collier had all her samples, and he had nobody left to charge. He was just escorting the valuable contents of an archaeological dig back to base. Collier said researchers would be arm-wrestling for the rights to it all.

"You know, I always feel a terrible sense of frustration when this happens," said Collier. She patted each little resin coffin carefully before sliding it into the cargo restraints. "Probably the last of their kind. There's so much we'll never know about them. You can really identify with lost races sometimes."

"Are you sure about that?" Reynolds asked. "That they're the last?"

"Pretty sure. If they had the technology to support space flight, we'd have found evidence by now. You've got a dozen survey teams here and all they've found is ruins and husks of shells. No, they were wiped out before we even knew they were there."

"What'll happen to the bodies?"

"Well, we'll treat them with due respect, preserve them in a dry chamber and divvy up the tissue samples and scans to universities."

"Not much of a memorial to an entire people."

"What we discover about them now will be as good a memorial as any. It's a kind of afterlife in its way."

Reynolds found it difficult, but he reached into his fatigues and took out the compact. It was even more jewel-like in the harsh illumination of the cargo bay, all dancing facets and engraving. It seemed to have stopped emitting sounds. Whatever it was – well, one day he would know. He handed it to Collier, and it hurt him to let it go.

"Somebody cared a lot about that," he said.

"Extraordinary work," Collier said, and accepted it without hesitation.

"Just sign for it to prove I didn't walk off with it, that's all. Can I check on what they find out about it?"

She smiled. "Of course."

"Thanks."

"Matters to you, doesn't it?"

"It belonged to someone, and they were murdered, and so were their kids. Things like that take on a significance."

His eyes couldn't break away from the compact as Collier handled it. "I suppose so," she said, and Reynolds was clear from her tone and her frozen frown of sympathy that he had said too much. "I'll leave you to finish up here."

He turned off all the lighting except the emergency panels and stood in silence. If he'd had a sincere prayer in him, he would have recited it, but he didn't, and taking these people away from home for the last time made him uneasy and in need of some ritual to appease his gut. He was going home to a wife and a new family. The crickets never would.

He walked round to each of the little resin containers, all neat and sealed and bone-dry inside, and touched each with his ungloved hands.

"Poor sods," he said, and closed the hatch behind him.

AN OPEN PRISON

(First published in *On Spec*, Winter 2003.)

> As an aid for paraplegic and quadriplegic patients, the Suit has a limited market. It has enormous potential as workwear in hostile environments, but the most lucrative application is as a replacement for the electronic tagging and incarceration of offenders. The one-off cost of a Suit is half the annual cost of keeping a criminal in a medium-security prison.
>
> (Marketing analysis, Carmody Life Engineering.)

It's pewter grey and slightly reflective and I have no idea why I've agreed to have this damn thing in my office. When I look at its skin, I expect it to be pneumatic and yielding like a vinyl beach-ball. It even smells like one. I don't want to touch it to find out.

There's a man inside it. What violence he's committed to end up encased in this all-encompassing correctional Suit, I mustn't ask: he has his privacy, which is why the Suit obscures his face – to protect him, not me.

All I know for sure is that this is not the man who

strangled my daughter. The prison service says it's very careful about that sort of thing.

"I'll be going now," says the man from Victim Support. "I'll drop by tomorrow. Anytime this gets too much for you, just call me." He takes his cell phone and infrareds his number into the phone on my desk. He must be able to see I'm on the edge. "And I mean *any* time."

So now I have a once-violent marionette in my office, standing frozen between the whiteboard showing orders of cat litter still to be dispatched and the browning *monstera deliciosa* I really ought to water properly. The figure is a parody of a 1940s cartoon robot: smooth and man-shaped, metallic as a gun, devoid of features other than the fencing-mask face and the body wastes bag moulded discreetly to the thigh. He has *chosen* this mobile form of incarceration. It's usually something reserved for low-risk prisoners – burglars, embezzlers, drunk drivers – so they can be active, useful but totally controlled while they serve their sentence.

But violence usually means life or the death penalty. Is prison so bad that he'd rather live out his time like this?

The anonymized creature can do nothing. If it wants to move, I have to release the Suit from its rigid lock. The device is more than an exoskeleton: the composite skin is bonded to its wearer and reaches down to control every major body system.

It can make you walk again. It can also hold you more captive than a prison cell.

Victim Support gives me one last look as if inviting me to say *no, take it away, get it out of here: I can't deal with this*. But I don't. And he leaves. I take a long look at the Suit. I can't make eye contact because I can't see the eyes, although I know the prisoner inside can see out.

I must be mad to have agreed to this. This is never going to help me come to terms with Sally's murder. Only causing savage and permanent pain to the man who killed her but didn't hang for it will achieve that: I have nursed that certainty for the last two years.

#

The Suit can be tailored for various hostile environments from marine to hard vacuum by the addition of appropriate materials to the nanoporous matrix. Energy generated in the exoskeleton can augment muscle power for workers handling heavy objects. For comfortable extended wear, the Suit can remove excreted matter at the same time as filtering out hazardous substances. But the Suit is equally at home in patient care, restoring mobility and independence in cases of paralysis and muscular weakness. Last year 15,000 stroke survivors suffering from dysphagia were able to enjoy solid food again thanks to the Suit, ending the need to feed via percutaneous endogastric tubes. The degree of control over movement and body functions afforded by the Suit also makes it ideal for the mobile incarceration of prisoners.

(News release, Carmody Life Engineering)

#

"Are you sure that thing's safe?" Valerie sticks her head round the door but doesn't seem to want to step into the office. She's my book-keeper. I sell wholesale pet products, the business that my husband Ray left to me because, like me, he couldn't cope with losing Sally. But he hung himself while I just wanted to lynch the whole world. Valerie has been an unexpected and solitary source of support. People I used to call friends avoid me now, not because they're embarrassed by bereavement but because I've turned into someone it's hard to be friends with.

Valerie needs convincing. "Nothing's going to go wrong, is it?"

"You've seen them sweeping streets. This one's no different." *Oh yes, he is*: the ones on civic pride duties have missed their child maintenance payments, or cheated the benefits system. This one has hurt or killed someone. "It – he can't get the Suit off, and the Suit won't let him do anything it's not programmed to do." I hold up the little handset control as if he's a TV. "He can't hurt us and we can't hurt him."

Damn. I've started saying *he* now.

"And how is this going to help you?" Valerie doesn't appear to be able to take her eyes off the figure. "You can knock ten bells out of him but it's not the man who killed Sally. It won't give you any release."

The Suit so artificial and featureless that I wonder if there's really a man inside after all. Maybe it's an automaton, a placebo, a harmless way of testing if being in control of a perpetrator can really help a victim. "It might not help me," I say. "But there's someone else out there that *he's* hurt. And maybe some other woman has the controls to the man who killed Sally. There's a sort of balance."

That's *not* the idea. I know that. There are only a handful of dangerous Suits out in the community, a pilot project to see if offenders can change if forced to face victims – to see if victims can change if they have the fate of an offender in their own hands.

That's what they tell the civil liberties lobby, anyway. Word gets round: one of the bastards rang me to rant about how I was colluding in human rights abuses by having the Suit around. I asked him what he thought of Sally's human right not to have the life squeezed out of her. He put the phone down.

We have a lot of orders to get out to pet stores today. That's the deal: Suits work for their keep. They don't run up prison bills. They don't break probation or parole, because the Suit can be tracked and immobilized. You don't even need guards, because the parks department or a company or whoever needs their labour does the supervision. They say the short-sentence Suits – the ones who sweep streets and weed old ladies' gardens – go home at night, still encased and controlled in that composite shell, but home nonetheless.

It's good economics. Does it provide justice for victims of crime? Maybe. Does it rehabilitate offenders? I don't give a damn. I pick up the handset and steer the metal-plastic thing out the door, towards the warehouse floor and onto the packing lines.

I put him in the line that's sealing up cardboard crates of assorted dog muzzles, sized from Yorkshire terrier to Doberman.

#

The Suit stops to eat when I say so. We go out to the loading bay where we have picnic tables for the staff to eat sandwiches when the weather's nice. By keying a code I allow the Suit movement in the arms and face, enough for the man inside to chew and swallow. It's a lovely sunny day, all high white wispy cloud; but most of the staff decide to eat elsewhere.

"Mel, how does it pee?" Valerie asks.

"Stores and dumps at the end of the day," I say. At night, he stays in the security office because it has a bed and a sink. "Like a spacesuit. It's self-cleansing." It's very clever, really, but maybe not the easy option for criminals that I once thought it was. The man inside is locked in it. He can't even speak unless I release the laryngeal implant. There's no taking a hacksaw to this particular wheel-clamp.

"They should tell you what he's done," Valerie says. She picks up fallen salad from her sandwich and stuffs it back inside the bread. "That way you know how to treat him."

"But if we know, then his victim finds out where he is, and all hell breaks loose." If I knew where Sally's murderer was, I would carry hell with me. "Better that we don't."

A thought appals me. I look at the giant Grey toy of a figure that's spooning lentil soup into its mouth. How do I know this *isn't* him? What if this is part of the experiment? What if the prison service has lied to me in some well-meaning attempt to save my feelings? I have to stop myself. After two years I should be past this madness – grieving, yes, but not still locked in crazy anger. Of course it's not him.

"Quite a deterrent," says Valerie.

"Being Suited?"

"Can't talk, can't eat, can't even pee except when your warder decides. That's worse than being in solitary. It'd make me think twice about breaking the law."

"Well, it didn't make him and lots of others pause for thought." He did something serious and destructive. I can't find pity anywhere in me. "Have you done this month's VAT returns?"

"Haven't totalled them yet. I'll close the books tomorrow." Valerie shakes the crumbs from her plastic sandwich bag for the sparrows to scavenge and puts it back in her jeans pocket. She recycles religiously. "I think we should call him John."

"If that makes you happier."

"Can't go round calling out 'Suit, come here Suit', can I? He needs a name."

He can only answer her summons when I allow him to anyway. But she's right. I want to punish this man. You can't punish a toy, a robot, a puppet. It has to be personal.

#

It's nearly time to go home. Fifteen cases of Dustfree KatLit have just left for the pet store in town, a late order. We always do our best to make late orders by the next working day, and I stay on later and later each week. I find it hard to go home to a house where my daughter and husband *aren't*. Their not being there is palpable: the house hasn't even got the decency to be empty.

On my desk, I have a picture of Sally when she was twelve. She's just learned to stay upright on ice skates. I look at it and often wonder what I would have felt or done or said then, had I known she had four years left to live. I'm not self-deluding; I know some of my rage-grief, a very small part, is driven by the fact that I didn't realise she had a secret life of her own at 16 and was meeting boys – men – I didn't know. I still don't know the full details. But one of them was Garry and he was 22 years old; he strangled her and left her behind the propane tanks at the tennis club.

I look at the picture again. Every time I do, I try to imagine what was going on in her mind in her last moments. I feel that by trying to experience it, I can take it away from her. But it never seems to work.

The Suit, John, is vacuuming the floor, so he's set on a reasonable degree of free physical movement. Don't worry: he can't hurt me because the Suit has inbuilt proximity sensors so that he'll be locked immobile before he can get too close to me. For his protection, the Suit is as good as a Kevlar jacket, proof against stabbing, bullet or blow. He stops raking the brush-head over the threadbare mock-Tientsin rug and his head is turned towards the photo.

He gestures with his hand towards the invoice pad on my desk, and picks up a pen. He's been here three months and I still don't want to hear his voice: this is the first time he's tried to communicate at all, and I have a burning split-second's cramp in my stomach because the thought of his helplessness is truly pitiful. I think of Sally and it passes, replaced by comfortable anger.

I let him take the pad. He writes awkwardly on it and hands it back.

Don't keep doing it to yourself. Your daughter only died once.

I have to stare at the unsteady writing for several seconds before it sinks in. Then I'm up out of my seat and running at him. My throat is snapped shut, the pressure is roaring in my ears and I'm in the second before a faint. John falls against the wall with a thud. I've just launched myself at him and knocked him to the ground, and the vacuum's motor dies into quiet as the power cable rips out of its socket.

I can't even manage to scream abuse at him, so visceral and all-consuming is my anger. I have to get out. I slam the door behind me and in my rush I almost forget to set the alarm. I have to go back and check it. I think of going back to my office and sorting John for the night, but I can't, and I don't want to, so I lock the handset.

I try to concentrate on my driving as I head home, unable

to shake the idea that it's *him* inside. This must be some idiot psychologist's idea of therapy. A safe confrontation, a sicker, sadder version of having the kid who stole your car come and mow your lawn for six months to say sorry. And then we'll all get on with our lives.

Another car's horn blares in a fading, mournful note as I stray across the centre line of the road. I really have to get a grip of this. It could end up killing me.

#

When I unlock the office the next morning and turn off the alarm, John is still lying where he fell. Last night I meant it and things were very clear. Now I'm not so sure. I've left him here all night, trapped and paralyzed in a kind of death. His Suit needs emptying; he smells of crap and urine. The last fourteen hours must have been unbearable for him, all discomfort and humiliation, and I find myself praying he really is the man who killed Sally.

That would make it all right.

"Come on," I say. "Go and clean up." I fumble with the handset and the Suit becomes fluid silver again, letting John stand up and totter unsteadily to the staff washroom. Having a constricting Suit that controls your every function doesn't stop you getting cramp, I suppose.

How like us, how like humans, to derive confinement from a technology originally designed to liberate. We turn everything to shit. And that's all I can smell.

"Just don't mention Sally again, okay?" I yell after him. "Don't talk about my daughter. You can't possibly know anything."

He's gone a long time. He can't have made a run for it, because the Suit reports in to a GPS system every few minutes. The prison service can even override my handset to immobilize him. But John eventually comes back and stands in my office as if he's waiting for orders.

"Go and help Brian get the plastic wrap off the bird

cages," I say. I look at the handset and leave it coded for free movement. "There's some bacon sandwiches and tea on the go in the kitchen."

Does the Suit record what happens to its occupant? Is the prison service going to send someone round to repossess John because I've taken a swing at him? They must know that's a risk because they use the protective version of the Suit, the sort for workers in hostile environments. I'm a hostile environment all by myself. For a while I sit wondering what it must be like to be sealed into a coating of silicon, metal and polymers. I try to imagine what it must feel like and all I can see is the shrink-wrapped cages waiting to be unwrapped in the warehouse.

I pick up Sally's picture and buff the chrome frame with my sleeve before putting it back at a slightly different angle so I can see it better. What would I do if I knew, absolutely knew, that the man in the Suit was the same one who killed her? I always thought I'd know exactly what I'd do, down to the last blow. Now I've got complete control over a violent offender, I feel guilt about leaving him lying all night with only his own excrement for company.

The psychologists think it can help me. They might even think it can help him. All I know is that his presence has created a whole new problem for me, that of being responsible for him in the smallest detail. This is a long way from the uncomplicated retribution that I work through in my head at three in the morning when I can't sleep.

As far as I'm concerned, the experiment has failed. I thought I'd be able to purge myself by facing a Suit and finally grieve properly. But he's the wrong Suit for the job.

They can take John away and let him do something useful in old ladies' gardens for all I care. I'll retreat into the comfortable world of my anger: I know the map.

#

Who is outraged by the prospect of criminals in Suits these days? I care more for the welfare and tax burden of the law-abiding majority than the care and resettlement of offenders. Suits have a comparable rate of recidivism to criminals serving jail sentences but cost the tax payer a great deal less. That is a successful policy by anyone's standards.

(Election address, Miles Jackson MP.)

#

Life never gets back to normal after you've lost someone, but you do establish an equilibrium. Mine is one of work, cheesecake and anger. Every Tuesday these days I take a couple of hours out during the morning after we've unloaded the regular bulk deliveries, and I sit in the coffee shop in the mall with a slice of cherry cheesecake and a mug of latte.

We used to enjoy that every Saturday morning after shopping for clothes, Sally and I, indulgent girly stuff. I have only been able to face the cherry cheesecake again – her favourite, my favourite – in the last couple of months. But I still can't face the happy, normal, nauseating crowds of Saturday shoppers: I resent their taken-for-granted family happiness. So quiet Tuesday morning is the most I can manage right now.

Nearby, a couple of Suits sweep the terrazzo flooring with programmed fluency. I haven't been this near to a Suit since John was taken back four years ago.

Their smooth anonymity doesn't bother me so much now. I've stopped playing the self-torturing I-spy game where I try to guess which one might be the man who killed Sally: I know he's serving life and that should be enough, even if I don't know if he's staring through bars now or peering through the face-plate of a Suit.

Tell me the stats again: ninety five per cent of Suits are not violent offenders. UnSuited, sentence served, they become human again and re-enter the world of people who can move and talk and eat as they please. I wonder if I'll ever be able to do that.

The coffee shop is on the ground floor of the atrium of

the complex. You can sit there and look up at people on the floors above like goods on shelves. And they can gaze down into the well of oversized pendant lights and coloured hanging banners. A bald middle-aged man in a pale blue sports shirt and taupe pants walks up to me as if he knows me. Maybe he's a customer: I have a bad memory for faces so I smile, just in case.

"Melanie Wilson?" he asks. I don't recognize the voice.

"That's me," I say.

"I'm Donald Belovich. You used to call me John."

It takes a couple of seconds for it to sink in, and he's already sitting down at my table. What should I say? Has he come to exact revenge? It's very public here so he if he attacks me, I can cry for help. I'm afraid. But that's only because I'm reminded of how vile I can be in my rages, how spiteful and sadistic. Now I can see his face and I know he's not the boy who killed Sally, I'm purged of all feelings towards him except shame and embarrassment.

"I know this is a shock," he says. "I thought a long time about this, but I got special permission to contact you now I'm out on license." He holds out his marked hand: he's micro-chipped like a valued pet dog for easy tracking. The few murderers who are released these days remain on license for the rest of their lives, liable to be jailed again for the most minor offence. It's another sort of Suit. "You need to know."

"Know that you didn't kill my daughter? Look, I'm sorry." I have to fill the gap. I don't want to let him be reasonable after the way I've treated him. "When you lose a child, you go crazy."

"I know," he says. "My daughter was run down and killed by a drunk. He got two year's probation plus a five year driving ban so I went to his house and put a screwdriver through his chest."

I sit motionless and remember.

I don't like revelation. I'm staring at the half-eaten wedge of cheesecake on my plate and all I can see is the contrast between the creamy whiteness and the cascade of impossibly scarlet cherry topping. *Your daughter only died once.*

"If I had known," I say at last, "I would never have reacted the way I did. I'm truly sorry."

"If you hadn't reacted like that, I wouldn't have learned that you can never get enough revenge."

Is he being clever? No, there's not a trace of humour on his face, just resignation. My expression must betray the horror I feel because he looks away as if embarrassed.

He feels *sorry* for me.

His pity is not because we have a shared tragedy. It's because I'm still consumed by attempting to erase events that can never be changed. I can see it.

"How did you find me?" I ask.

"From Valerie. I went back to the warehouse." He lowers his eyes as if he's confessed something terrible. "She thought it wouldn't do you any harm to talk to me."

I wish she hadn't told him. But he would have made contact anyway, somehow. And maybe Valerie knows what I need to hear better than I do sometimes.

"Was it...bad in the Suit?" I ask. Oh God, that's feeble: but what words do you choose with a man you've tortured? "I can't imagine."

"I nearly went insane," he says.

I'm not proud of feeling reassured by that. I'm reassured not by the fact that it was purgatory for him, but that the man who killed Sally may be going through the same claustrophobic agony. I try not to feel that throat-blocking nausea when I realise that I vented my rage on a man who had simply done what I longed to do; to make someone pay an appropriate price for my child's death.

"I can move on now," he says. "Don't feel bad about it. I needed the shock of being alongside you. A mirror for what was eating me up."

He shifts towards the edge of the chair. If I ever see him again in the street, I'm not even sure I'll recognize him. Then he puts his hand briefly on my arm, something the Suit would never let him do. "Thank you." He gets up and walks a few paces, then stops and turns. "I mean it. Thank you. Now live your life. Your daughter wouldn't have wanted to see you spend the rest of your life like this."

He's been gone about ten minutes now. I ask myself what I'd do if the next man to walk up to me were the man who killed Sally. I know as surely as I know anything that I would not hesitate to fling myself at him and tear and punch and claw.

Forgiveness is something that only Sally can bestow. I have no right to forgive. But John has stepped out of his Suit.

And I have yet to escape from mine.

CHOCOLATE KINGS

(First published in *On Spec*, Fall 2002. Honourable mention, Year's Best Science Fiction #20 Written as an exercise at Clarion East workshop, 2000. If memory serves, the test was to pick an obscure topic, and someone tasked me to write about chocolate.)

Some people – well, some people just deserved to be child sacrifices, and Superintendent Nuataxtl was one of them. He had the timing of a sadist. There we were, filing away our last crime reports for the day and just waiting for the sun to dip below the horizon, and in he came. There was no getting out that door now.

"The mezcal bar's going to miss you tonight, Ahuatl," he said. "In fact, it might be missing you tomorrow night too. All of you. You've just got to see what Customs turned over at the airport."

Now, the appeal of the Commercial Branch – a.k.a. Fraud Squad – to half-hearted detectives like me was that you usually worked business hours: no night surveillance, no armed blags and no resisting arrest. (Although I did nick a very stroppy accountant last season, and those little bean-counters can put up a hell of a fight.) And faster promotion, too, because most coppers didn't consider fraud-busting to be real men's work. It was a good way to get a desk job at HQ – if you fancied working in the Big Temple, that is.

This wasn't a desk job night. "Sergeant, we have forensics squad on its way and you'll take the mobile assay team with you," said Nuataxtl. "We're talking big haul here, my son. Headline stuff."

"Tobacco?" I asked. They got excited about illegal tobacco, although I couldn't work out why people drank the stuff. "How much?"

"No, counterfeit xocolatl. Five tons of it. And guess where it's come in from?"

"No idea, Super."

"Some freeze-arse state called Helvetia."

It was what we had all dreaded. The Europeans had found a way to fake chocolate. It wasn't just our economy that was at stake.

It was our whole way of life.

#

Don't get me wrong. I've got nothing against Europeans. I mean, if they weren't cleaning the hotels and driving the buses, we'd have to do it. But they liked easy money. My mate Kahpua (a bit of a liberal) reckoned they were driven to crime because the respectable jobs like architecture, priesting and chocolate production weren't open to them.

But this particular job wasn't easy money. It was high tech. Believe me, when I got out the squad car and walked across that runway to the cargo plane, it was like stepping onto a film set. There were hi-lux arc lights and cordons and sniffer dogs going bananas, whining and leaping around because they could smell something and couldn't reach it.

A thin lad in a Customs uniform was walking towards me in that way that said he was trying to intercept, but I wasn't going to stop. We almost collided. He whipped out his obsidian badge and flourished it. I pulled out my big jade one.

"Piss off, son," I said, as kindly as I could. "This is police business now."

I shoved past him and began looking for a technician. I only spotted the senior forensics officer from the fact that it said SFO in really big letters on the back of his high-visibility tabard. Otherwise he'd just have been another bloke in a white noddy suit with a mask on, like the rest of the crowd swarming round the plane. I didn't need to ask why he needed the mask. As soon as I got close enough, I could smell it.

There was the meaty, bitter tang of the pure-grade xocolatl, and then the – well, there was only one way to describe it. The stench of cheap vanilla made me want to throw up.

I actually heard Kahpua gag behind me.

"Oh, fucking Feathered Serpent, Sarge, that's *disgusting*," he said. Normally I'd have stuck him on a charge for blaspheming, but I had to agree with him. It didn't smell like any chocolate I'd ever come across. And I'd handled it all at the Imperial Mint during training: bars, beans, 50% ground, fine ground, right up to the pure stuff.

"Can I see it?" I asked the SFO.

"You're looking at it," he said, well muffled, and spread his arms to reveal a big smear of brown grease down his chest like someone had crapped on him. He pulled the mask down from his face. He talked as best anyone could when they were trying to hold their breath. "They've packed every double-skinned wall on the aircraft with it."

I looked at the plane again. It was a tatty little tin can, with brown rust stains along every riveted seam. The bright arc lights didn't flatter it much. I was amazed it had survived a five thousand mile journey.

"So, they blew it in like insulation?" I asked.

SFO rolled his eyes in exasperation and pushed the mask back on his face to suck in a bit of cleaner air. "No, they poured it in, you moron," he said. "In liquid form. That's not rust. It's chocolate leaking out the bloody seals. Don't you people talk to Customs? This is the fifth consignment we've had through this year. It's just a lot more than usual, that's all."

I would normally *not* take kindly to being called a moron, but I was distracted by the suggestion that those secretive bastards in Customs should have briefed us. We'd have a word with them later. Poured? Poured what? And then the xocolatl bean dropped, as my mum would have said.

"It's frozen in a water suspension?" I asked, trying to look like I'd paid attention in chemistry class.

"No."

SFO handed me a disposable paper mask and led me over to the tail end of the plane, where they'd set up a screened area. There were blokes in coveralls – and masks, of course – trying to funnel a shiny, slimy, stinking ooze of brown stuff from an opening in the tail section into big metal drums.

"They're bloody clever for Euros," SFO said. "We've worked it out. They mix the chocolate solids and oils they can get hold of with vegetable fat – about forty per cent dilution, I'd say – toss in fake vanilla substitute, and bulk it out with something they call sugar. Now that's a pretty inert monosaccharide compound they get from beets."

"Oh yeuch…"

"You haven't heard the worst yet. Some of the stuff is a bit on the light side, colour wise, and I've known them add a burned version of the monosaccharide called caramel so it looks as dark as the real thing. When it's cold, it sets solid."

He took a plastic sample tub from his tabard and shook it: it rattled like pure stuff. And then he took my hand (yeah, I know, but I was mesmerised by then) and tipped a couple of shiny beans into my palm.

They looked like the real thing. And then they began to soften and spread in the heat of my hand and I actually watched them turn into that brown gunk.

"This stuff," said SFO, "has been turning up all over the Empire. And you can pass a lot of it off in cooler places before it's spotted."

"How was it getting past Customs, then?"

"Easy. It's brown. It's runny. They were putting it in false lavatory tanks on board and letting the sanitation wagon pump it out and take it away for collection and remoulding later."

I'd forgotten about Kahpua. He was right behind me, and I turned to look at him. He was pretty dark-skinned, but he was definitely looking ashen right then. I turned back to SFO. "So is there a quick test for this stuff?"

"Oh, you just taste it," he said, and dabbed his tongue onto the brown-smeared palm of his protective glove.

I heard Kahpua's rapid sprint away from us and into the bushes. He never did have much of a stomach on him.

#

We got our faces on the news (and we elbowed in front of those Customs bastards, too) but it wasn't enough to brag about a five ton haul. We were under pressure to stop the counterfeit currency coming in. Sniffer dogs were one thing, but the politicians wanted to know why we had to pay to stop those Helvetics from undermining our economy. Wasn't there a way of tackling the influx at source?

We had a meeting about it. We didn't like meetings much, but I thought I'd better learn to get good at them if I had delusions of promotion. The senior Customs officers lined up opposite us, all smarting from the row over who had jurisdiction.

"Come up with an idea," said the Commissioner.(A big bloke. I mean *really* big.) "One that doesn't involve bombing Helvetia back to the stone age, although it hasn't got that far to go from what I hear. We've been warned off being too heavy on emerging nations. You know, we've got all the chocolate, the World Bank, etcetera etcetera and bleeding heart etcetera."

He had placed a pile of the counterfeit 40% pure in the centre of the big polished stone conference table to concentrate our minds. I really did like that room: turquoise inlays up the walls, decorative crystal skulls on dinky little pedestals and a ceremonial seat at the end of the chamber. It gave HQ a nice traditional Aztec feel. All you needed was the priest and the obsidian dagger and we would have been back in the good old days, when we weren't being buggered about by the third world.

"We can impose trade sanctions," said a Customs officer.

"They don't buy anything from us," the Commissioner said. "They can't afford it. Next?"

"We could choke their xocolatl supply at source."

"No-o-o, we can't starve them of currency. Empire Bank and all that."

I was still staring at the various shiny fakes on the cool table. They were holding shape pretty well, and the shapes were whatever they'd managed to pour the liquid into when they were scrambling to collect it – cups, bars, knobbly shapes, even a pudding mould. It seemed a strange thing to do with chocolate. There was powdered chocolate for drinking (with water, honey and a real vanilla pod, of course) and chocolate for spending (cultivated regular, uniform size) and there was investment chocolate, selectively cultivated for huge beans and whacking high theobromine and caffeine content.

But bars? Globes? *Shapes?*

And then it hit me.

Sometimes, just sometimes, you get those flashes from nowhere, right out of the dark earth. Clever buggers get those all the time, but ordinary blokes like me get them once in a lifetime. When you get one, you've got to grab and make it work for you.

"We could sell it back to them," I said.

There was a silence. I didn't know if it was a ooh-he's-clever silence, or a who-let-him-in-here silence. I looked round all those rigid jaws and narrowed eyes and wondered if I'd said goodbye to inspector rank right there and then.

"Do you want to expand on that?' said the Commissioner.

No, I didn't: not really. But there was a bigger jade badge at the end of this tunnel. All I had to do was dig.

"Well, it tastes odd, but when it's solid you can chew it," I said. "National tastes vary. There are people in Europe who like rotted milk. In big lumps. So who's to say we couldn't get one of the food companies to tart this up a bit and market it back to them?" I was on a roll. The gods were right there with me. "We could put almonds in it. All sorts of things. We could make it into shapes, like eggs and mountains and things. Then we tell them how good it is, and they have to pay for it from their xocolatl reserves, so we gradually shift the balance of xocolatl back here."

The Commissioners big face lit up. "You really do want that inspector's badge badly, don't you, son?" he said. "Let me put that idea forward. It's got everything. It's politically sound, it might even show a profit, and it'll teach those Helvetic types a lesson." He pushed the stool back from the table with an *eeeek* of stone against tile. "And if it fails, we can say it was the deranged idea of a junior officer."

"Thank you, sir," I said.

#

Kahpua and I sat in the mezcal bar when the shift had ended. It was the same most nights: we filed the reports for the day, and then went and got pissed as handcarts. (Yes, I know, wheels: the Europeans did have their moments.) Except this night I took my inspector's jade badge out of the fob inside my jacket and slapped that on the bar in front of me.

"Two pints of your finest, Freddie boy," I said to the pasty-faced little Euro polishing the glasses. "I'm celebrating. And have one for yourself."

"How did you get the idea?" Kahpua asked.

"It was looking at the shapes. That's all. Just reminded me of cakes and sweets. It's what they call an intuitive leap."

"Still can't look at the stuff," he said. "Why the almonds?"

"If they try to smuggle it back to us, the little gritty bits will be easy to spot. And they'll clog up their machinery." I had to laugh. "It's the eggs and the tile-shaped ones I like best."

"Seriously, though, you think they'll fall for it? That this stuff is worth buying?"

"Don't underestimate Aztec marketing ingenuity," I said. "There'll be a novelty market for a while, and then they'll get the message. Don't mess with the Aztec fraud squad."

I looked up at the mirror-backed bar, between the bottles and badges and memorabilia garnered from year upon year of Mexico City police officers who drank here. It was a bit of a black museum, really, stacked with objects liberated surreptitiously or otherwise from investigations – deactivated firearms, the odd obsidian blade, and a jar of unidentifiable dried-out stuff that was probably from a path lab.

And then there was the newest addition to the collection: one of my chocolate bars, the one shaped like a piece of square-tiled floor. I looked at it and felt a little sad, shiny new jade badge or not.

"No," I said. "I don't think it'll ever really catch on."

A SLICE AT A TIME

(First published in *Asimov's*, July 2002. Honourable mention, Year's Best Science Fiction #20. Written as an exercise at Clarion East workshop, 2000.)

It was stress, the psychiatric report said, that had driven the mother to eat her two youngest children. There was nothing to be achieved by prosecuting her.

"But these were healthy youngsters," Nick said. "There was nothing wrong with them at all."

He closed the report on screen. It wasn't the first time the resident aliens on Maran V had eaten their offspring, but it was unusual for them to eat healthy ones. It was the first time in his stint as senior social worker at the Taranto colony that he'd actually dealt with a cannibalism case.

"What do you think, Ian?"

The trainee social worker he had acquired for the year was crammed in the corner of the twenty-five square meter office. He shrank behind a desk that had seemed a good idea in the catalogue but had been a little too large on arrival, and nobody in the department was prepared to pay the exorbitant freight charges to ship it back to base. The kid had a fixed wide-eyed expression, as if he'd been freeze-dried in the middle of seeing something terrible.

"Ian? In a case like this, would we recommend prosecution or would be ask the court for a supervision order?" It was a policy thing, a matter of judgement, and if Ian was going to make it in this job he would have to take those decisions on his own one day. "Well?"

"Culturally sensitive area," Ian said in a mechanical tone. "Minimum intervention, seek regular client meetings to ensure the safety of offspring still living in the family home."

"Spot on."

Nick had forgotten what it was like to be new to the job: he'd made sure he had. "They take some getting used to, the ussissi," he said. "But give it a year and they'll look just like human clients."

"I'll take your word for it," said Ian.

"Remember you're seeing the atypical members of their species."

"I'll remember that, too."

"We'll need to carry out a home visit ourselves, and then we can file recommendation formally to the court." Nick topped up his coffee from the dispenser and took a very dry cracker out of the packet in his desk drawer. "The key factor here is that the shrink thinks the underlying causes of the cannibalism have eased."

"Meaning?"

"The mother was under a great deal of stress because of the new male in the household. There's always some adjustment. In this case she snapped."

"Twice?"

"We can regard it as one incident. The children were within months of each other in age, and you have to bear in mind they were very young, just within the range where a mother would make the decision to destroy them if they were defective. The remaining children are much older."

Ian was rotating his coffee beaker on the tabletop and looking forlorn. Nick held out the packet of crackers to him, but he shook his head. "That's all right then," he said, and Nick wasn't sure if he meant it.

The kid would get things in perspective, given time.

#

The drive over to the ussissi part of the settlement took half an hour, not because of the distance but because it took time to exit the human compound, with its sealed atmosphere and G-class full spectrum lighting. Nobody went off-camp without a back-up supply of air and water. It wasn't a poisonous atmosphere, just low on oxygen. And it wasn't an arid region, but the local water wasn't quite drinkable if left untreated. It wasn't even a hostile world. Just far enough away from freely habitable to remind men that they were invaders.

The ussissi managed to live in it comfortably, though. They always said it was so much better than the place they left.

Nick drove out into gently undulating landscape which would have looked like downland had it not been for the yellow daylight and the greyish vegetation. It gave the place a permanent look of impending storms. But Ian was of the generation born in this colony so – Nick supposed – the red sun looked normal and the yellow light suggested not storm but another pleasant day.

"I didn't believe they really did that," Ian said.

"Did what?"

"Ate their young. Like rabbits. I thought it was just one of those stories."

"You locals don't have much contact with them, do you?"

"No. I knew the ate their elderly, though."

Nick wanted to turn to look at the boy, but he found it hard to steer without his eyes fixed on the dirt-track road. "They only eat youngsters when they're defective in some way. They eat their elderly as a matter of course when they get too frail or ill."

"I think it's going to take a lot longer than a year for me to treat them just like us."

"Have you worked with human clients yet?"

"Not many."

"Ever seen an old people's home?"

"No. That's an Earth thing."

"Or tried to fathom parents who've systematically battered their baby?"

Ian didn't reply, and Nick wasn't sure if he was intimidated by the challenge or just out of words for the day. He drove on in silence.

Ussissi had their own cultural values. It wasn't for humans to intervene unless the creatures broke their own laws or interfered with humans. *A care home inspection. The stench of shit and an old woman tied to a chair to stop her wandering around.* It was an agreement reached when the ussissi asked to site a colony on the planet long after the humans first claimed it: human jurisdiction with respect for cultural differences, as long as those differences stayed within their respective settlements. *A post mortem on a six-month old baby. Fourteen healed fractures of ribs, skull and femur, seriously malnourished, skin ulcerated through neglect, and a mother who never, ever saw her boyfriend hurt the kid.*

There were worse things than being eaten.

"Put your oxygen on," said Nick. "Nearly there."

#

A home visit to a ussissi family meant a meeting in a communal hall. The chambers where the families lived were too small by a metre all round for a human to negotiate comfortably, and the creatures were usually understandably agitated by the dominating presence of a large human in their quarters. The communal hall gave everyone a little safe space.

It smelled wrong: it was dry, very dry, but the place smelled as wet and fungal as a forest. Even with the oxygen mask on, Nick could still taste a scent not unlike the woodland round his childhood home. And there the similarity ended.

The three ussissi parents huddled in a group, the two

smaller ones either side of the larger "mother". Nick squatted down on his haunches and Ian followed suit. Everyone exchanged non-hostility gestures as best they could, and Nick placed the flat, hand-sized portable translator on the ground between them.

"Our doctor thinks your children should stay with you." Nick waited while the software translated in thin tones from its small speakers: simple words stood less chance of misinterpretation. "A human will visit you every seven cycles to see that everything is alright. Are you willing?"

Nick waited. It was hard to communicate with a creature without eyes. Strictly speaking, that wasn't true: ussissi could see, but their sensors weren't committed to two points like a human's. They were spread all over the head. Combined with the identifiable mouth – that needle-ringed, vivid, cartoon-caricature mouth – it gave ussissi an appearance of savage hairless little animals.

The mother emitted a series of high-pitched grunts. Nick had no idea what other sounds there might be, out of the range of his hearing. "I agree. I want children to stay." The translator paused. "I regret. I regret."

The men eased themselves back on to their feet, Ian with more grace than Nick.

Without warning, there was a sound from one of the chambers: a sudden, sharp infant squeal that went right off the scale and left them pressing their ears, and then ended abruptly. Nick didn't need an interpreter to understand it. Ian made an involuntary move in the general direction, but the older man put a restraining hand on his arm.

"None of our business, remember?"

"Nick!"

"We respect their cultural differences. They're technological, organised, literate. Not animals. Just different."

All the way back to the colony, Ian said nothing, nothing at all. It was a long time before he spoke again.

#

For a social worker, Taranto Colony was as near to Shangri-La as anywhere was ever going to get. The population was still small, well educated, fit and pretty well socially homogeneous. There was no under-class, not yet. It didn't make any difference to the wife-beating and child abuse and neglect of the elderly, of course. It was just a smaller caseload. But that suited Nick fine.

Whether it suited Ian was another matter, and Nick had his doubts. The boy didn't seem to be settling. It was six months in to his probationary period, and he was still taking things far too personally.

"You have to learn to let go, kid," Nick told him. "What's normal for you isn't normal for other families. And it's definitely not normal for ussissi."

Ian wasn't making serious work of his sandwich. He was a thin, freckled boy and he looked like he needed to eat. Nick preferred women on the team: they were a lot tougher. They built thick skins very easily. But Ian was as raw to the touch as ever.

"Nick, you've been here ten years, right?" he said.

"Six years on Earth, ten here."

"And you prefer here?"

"I prefer here." *Don't do a home visit with a potentially violent client on your own, take back-up. One of you stays in the car at all times. Sarah's been a long time in there. Is she okay? Oh, God...* "Definitely, I prefer here."

"Why do we even get involved with aliens?"

"It's not benevolent. It's precautionary because it's less provocative to keep an eye on them through a social worker than through the military."

Ian looked as if he were chewing the idea over, which was more than he was doing with the sandwich. It was as close as Nick had been able to get to a heart-to-heart with him. Then he raised his eyes. His expression was surprising: Nick had expected to see something that would make him want to reassure the kid, but instead there was pity.

Pity, and a little revulsion.

"You don't see it, do you?" Ian said.

"We're not manipulating them. We respect their —"

"It's nothing to do with the aliens. It's us."

"I don't get it."

"It's crept up on you, hasn't it? A slice at a time. You've got so used to things by degrees that you can't see wrong for what it is."

"You can't take things too hard in this line of work. It'll burn you out."

"That's got nothing to do with the basic issue." He was the manifestation of clarity and youthful conviction now, not the thin ginger-haired geek who looked like he needed teaching about Life. "We rationalise so we can convince ourselves that what we see isn't wrong. That's what gets me. That's how we get to treat it as normal, by taking it in small doses. Makes evil easier to swallow, right?"

His voice cut off as if he'd left the room. Instead he was still sitting there, silent, and he began biting into the sandwich. Nick was unprepared to fill the gap.

"It's not all bad stuff," he said at last. "We support the elderly, we help people get back to work after illness. There are plenty of good things to see in this job." *Sarah, not quite herself after months in hospital, speech permanently slurred from a fractured skull, never able to work again.* "You have to think of all the things we do that aren't dealing with the dregs."

"Really?" Ian finished his sandwich and his expression said that he would no longer believe anything Nick would say. "And that balances the books?"

"Ian, I came into this job thinking I could put things right, but in the end you just have to do the best you can. How can I moralise about these creatures eating their disabled kids when I've seen what human parents do? You think that's any better? At least ussissi don't batter and rape them."

"No, they eat them, and it doesn't happen every day, but they do it just the same."

"Okay, say we take these infants into care. I tried that,

once, with this little thing that couldn't walk, and we fed it and kept it alive. But it could never be accepted by its own society and we ended up trying to stop it bashing its own head against the wall for hours because it was so isolated and terrified."

"And what happened to it?"

"We returned it to its family. Yes, I knew what would happen. And no, I couldn't save the whole bloody world, so I just did my best."

Nick was suddenly embarrassed at his outburst. Ian stared back at him, a total contrast in his flat cold disapproval. No, he would probably never listen to a boss again.

Nick went back to his screen and tried to recall happy old ladies settled in new assisted housing, icons of dignified, independent old age.

But he couldn't. Not right then.

#

Taranto was a pleasant colony, no doubt about it. Nick sat in the green, rustling atrium at the heart of the complex and enjoyed ginger tea and a news download. You could play god in a colony. If you wanted translucent dendrobiums cascading from bark above the shops, you could, and you could have strelitzias in the borders, and apricot trees in fruit, and it didn't matter at all that the main purpose of the vegetation was that you needed ten square metres of it to provide renewable oxygen for one human. There was more to life than breathing.

Sometimes it was hard to appreciate the small good detail in life. Nick tried hard to keep in practice, because as surely as he managed to shut out the demons, he had shut out the angels, too. It got harder over the years. The door didn't discriminate: he kept it shut.

He wandered back down the colonnade which ran alongside a miniature artificial river, and a weir built solely to create the sound of rushing water. One day he would come back and enjoy this when he had time. Did ussissi ever come here? He'd only seen a handful inside the settlement, and those looked to be on official business. There was nothing stopping them entering – not yet. They just didn't come.

When he got back to his office there was a note waiting for him on the messaging system. It was from Ian. It spoke of his regret that he had to resign, but he felt he would be happier doing an administration job in the planning department. He had an interview later that week, so would Nick mind doing a reference for him? Nick didn't mind at all. The lad wasn't really suited for social work.

And Nick didn't need his reminders that there were things to which he was determined to be blind. Life would get back to normal now.

#

There were no trainees for the next four months, but there wasn't much of a caseload either, so Nick felt no pressure. He had time to complete admin work and proposals for the first time in ages. The phone didn't ring much either; he could have the video link on during office hours to watch the news. It was all pretty comfortable.

He kept thinking that right up to the time the receptionist buzzed him and said there was an ussissi in an agitated state at the front desk, unable to make much use of the translator but insistent on "Nick, Nick, Nick".

"I'll see her," he said, because he knew there was only one ussissi who would make the journey and ask for him personally. He went out to show her in.

And he was wrong.

It wasn't the cannibal mother. It was a much older female, and he could tell that from the dark colour of her shark-skin limbs. She fell against the furniture as she came in, an eyeless sloth with a cartoon mouth of teeth. The high-pitched squeals were almost painful. He stood back and let her circle the room unsteadily until she came to an exhausted halt, flanks heaving.

Nick got down on all fours and edged up close enough to her to get the translator between them so they could both reach it.

"I'm Nick," he said. "What's your name?"

A pause, and shrills came out of the machine. "Ressi."

"What's wrong?"

"Die, die, die."

"Someone's dead?"

"Me. I die."

For a moment he thought she was ill. He knew little about ussissi physiology. Then he looked at the age of her, the charcoal skin, her unsteady gait, and the picture focused sharply in his head. She was old. It was her time to die, and she hadn't died on time.

"Are you afraid?"

"I will not die."

"Your family wants to ... eat you?"

"I will not die." The creature put her little clammy three-fingered paw on his forearm. He never could understand why creatures who could live in such an arid world felt and smelled so damp. "Help me."

"What can I do?"

"Help me."

"I'm not allowed to interfere with your laws."

"Help me. Help me." A pause. "Nick."

He never took things too personally. But she had made it personal. It was as if she had bound him to the problem simply by invoking his name. And he suddenly saw a frightened old lady cowering before him.

#

"Nick, you can't keep the thing there."

"She's a client."

"Yes, and her family want her back. You can't interfere."

"Jesus Christ, Sanjay, they're going to eat her. Have you

thought what that means? They kill her and eat her. It's not even a lethal injection."

"It's their culture. We have a non-interference agreement."

"Oh yeah, and because it's her culture she's perfectly happy with it? Then why is she in here begging me to save her?"

"You really need to consider your position."

Nick killed the audio for a few moments and sat looking at his manager's face on screen. Then he glanced across at Ressi, who was curled up in the corner, dozing, with the remains of a plate of greens in front of her. It was the only thing he could find in the office fridge that she would eat. She'd been in his office two days now.

"I'm really uncomfortable with this," he said. "I have a professional code of ethics I have to follow. A vulnerable client has specifically asked for my protection. What the hell do you expect me to do?"

"Stick to the rules," said Sanjay. "Don't interfere in families when you don't have to."

"I try not to." *No, I don't think we should take the kid into care or prosecute the father. We shouldn't break families up. It's common in rural areas for fathers to screw their daughters.* "I really do try."

"You've got to talk her into going back. Her family are furious. There's a lot of ill-feeling in the ussissi community about this."

"And the administration is keen to see this resolved."

"This isn't the time or place for big ethical gestures, Nick." *Don't break the family up.* "When might that time be, then?"

"Don't piss around. Just do it, okay?"

It's what they do in these communities. "I'll think about it."

Nick shut off the link and thought about Ian. He hoped the kid was happier now, processing plans for new domes and fine colonnades. Right now he could have done with his certainty, the certainty born of a clear, uncompromised view of things as they really were. *Evil got you a slice at a time.* Ian never had the time to build up layer upon layer of the coping lies you needed to pretend to yourself that you weren't complicit in something very, very bad. He just saw the beast for itself.

Nick watched Ressi sleeping and wondered if he had been an evil man. No, he couldn't accept that. Had he done bad things? Yes. Stupid, inexcusable things, if you looked in from the outside. *Fathers screw their daughters here. It's not as bad as you think.* Why had he shut it all out? Because that was what professionals did, and that was what objective people did.

That was also what cowards did.

He didn't want that door in his head to open, but memory forced the lock and he remembered how he would deal with the undealable as a child. Not understanding what glue mousetraps were. Having his father explain it to him. Finding his breath temporarily jammed in his throat, and then imagining the terror and slow misery of the mouse. Finding the image so terrible that it jumped out at him at random moments, and the only way he could stop the insistent pain in his heart was to see it over and over and over again until it had lost all meaning, and he could sleep again.

Evil had a stealth all its own.

Ressi stirred. She turned her head towards him. "I not die. You help."

He didn't know if it was a question or a statement. The machine wasn't efficient at inflections. "I help," he said.

#

Nick tried to tell Sanjay that this wasn't like trying to save a youngster. All Ressi wanted was to die in her own time, and when she had, the family could have the body. But Sanjay wasn't giving way; the non-interference agreement had to stand, and Ressi would be taken back to her family one way or another. Nick cut the video link.

There was nothing about the incident on the news, perhaps because ussissi didn't use the media and humans didn't give a damn. But Nick locked the doors to his office just in case. On day four he sent the receptionist home and asked her to divert emergency calls to the health service.

He could sit it out; he had a couple of weeks' supply of food and access to a washroom. In a few days Sanjay would realise he meant business, and then they would find somewhere to accommodate Ressi in her final days. She was just one old lady. How difficult could it be?

He was wrong. After eight days the administration lost their patience with him and four troopers kicked down his office door. It happened fast and methodically. One snatched up Ressi from the pile of cushions on the floor and the others pinned Nick against the wall.

It made him glad that it took all three of them to hold him and that the only way they stopped him punching free was a rifle butt to the head. It didn't knock him cold: movies lied. *Sarah, in a pool of her own blood, just breathing. I warned you never to take chances with unstable clients.*

He could still hear everything around him.

The high warbling scream faded with a touch of Doppler down the corridor. There was no point yelling "Ressi" after her, because she couldn't have understood, but he did it anyway. He yelled for all the times he'd never yelled. He yelled for all the times he wanted to punch an abuser and never knew it. He yelled until his guts hurt.

The faces above him were blurred and their voices, shot with panic, merged into one stream of sound. "We'll get a medic mate, take it easy – Christ, why did you hit him that hard? – I'm sorry, mate, I know how tough it must be – Will they fire him for this?"

Nick no longer cared. He could see everything again. Evil couldn't sneak up on him or cut him a slice at a time any more. The door was open, and the devils had burst through, but they weren't alone.

There were a few angels behind them. He'd get to know them in time.

STRINGS

(First published in *Realms of Fantasy*, October 2002.
Honourable mention, Year's Best Science Fiction #21)

Let me tell you this: I never even *liked* Orpheus.

You should never believe what you read in mythology. The stories are true, of course, at least in part. But they're written down by the fallible, translated by the inept, perpetuated by people with axes to grind.

And told by men.

So if you teach classics, or if you care about the truth in any way at all, tell your children this – Eurydice didn't love Orpheus for all eternity.

In fact, I hated him.

#

Picture this: I'm fourteen. The whole village, the whole nation, is enthralled by the musical skills of Orpheus. Whatever I feel for him now, I have to concede that his talent was every bit as magical as the myth said. And I was the prettiest girl in the region, food for heroes, or so I thought.

You might have heard I was a dryad or a nymph. I think something was lost in the translation, because I was – am – a mortal. But it probably seemed less glamorous to have the fabulously talented son of Apollo and Calliope drooling after a merchant's daughter, pretty or not, so in retelling I have been part-deified. Or perhaps it was the olive trees. Yes, I did spend a lot of time with those trees, because my family's livelihood depended on them.

Orpheus, luring humans and animals and even rocks with his lyre, glanced briefly at me in the *agora* and I did indeed feel like a goddess for a few moments. Then he glanced away again.

He went on playing a slow cascade of pure notes that trickled like water down the scale. I felt the sounds deep in my body like a missed heartbeat, as if it would never beat again: and yet it did, and it seemed to beat to the slow rhythm of his music. It left a yearning void in my chest but it was not unpleasant or frightening, merely a longing like recalling a happy time long gone. I could have held it in me forever.

Everyone in the *agora* had stopped what they were doing. A woman in a grubby yellow gown paused while tying bunches of green chick-pea pods: two men haggling loudly over a bolt of dalmatic cloth fell silent at exactly the same time as the grasshoppers and bees did. The notes hung in the still, hot air.

The world stopped for Orpheus. It always did.

He plucked away at the strings, staring down at them as if oblivious of the fact that he had suspended time, and then stopped and looked up. A second of absolute silence: and then everyone clapped and laughed, and he had the grace to bow his head and grin. My heart assumed its usual rhythm. Market-day life in the *agora* could continue again. Even the scrubby wild thyme tumbling from the walls, tempted a few hand-spans forward by his music, appeared to recede again like a tide.

My friend Metis giggled and lowered her voice, evidently unable to stop staring at Orpheus, who was now surrounded by adoring women from little girls to grandmothers in black. "Isn't he wonderful? Isn't he just everything you've ever longed for?"

I had to admit she was right. That music was irresistible, and so was he. He had something about him, something beyond being a young man, and I glanced at him hoping for another look from him. And I got it, and my day had meaning. It was the kind of magic you could work if your mother was a muse. But it was the kind of magic that an oil-merchant's daughter, even a pretty one, could only observe.

There was another girl watching him intently. When she turned to watch him pass, I saw she was heavily pregnant, weeping quietly, and I thought she was about to approach him for something. But he didn't even look at her. She watched him go and wandered off into the market.

A few days later they found a pregnant woman dead at the foot of the cliffs. I wondered if it was her. I never asked.

#

I admit I had a crush on Orpheus. Everyone – *everything* – did. On market days Metis and I would stand near the front of the rapt crowd – not *at* the front, you understand, nothing so forward – to get a better look as Orpheus played. I was as mesmerized as anyone by the beautiful, shivering liquid notes of the lyre, but to this day I can't actually recall any of the tunes.

He stopped and we all resumed living again, bathed in a wonderful sensation of euphoric warmth and half-formed happy memories. Then he walked slowly and deliberately over to me and the group of women around me parted like grain. "Today it's you I play for," he said. "You deserve my music."

He put his hand carefully against the side of my face. Yes, I know: it was breathtakingly arrogant. I should have slapped him. I would have, had I been the woman that I am now. But I didn't. I *couldn't*. The music built up every time me every I heard it and slowly bathed away almost every doubt, every fear, every thought that wasn't him. But I could still see that pregnant girl, and I wondered if she would have my own face one day.

He bowed his head and grinned, and walked back through the women while pausing to look them over. He focused on me once more. "We shall be together," he said.

If you'd heard we had eyes only for each other, you were very much mistaken.

#

It was autumn and the olives were ripe enough to beat from the trees. We gathered them up in baskets, some for curing in lye and some for crushing into oil, great tubs of green and gold and purple-black fruits. It was a family day. My mother and father, my grandmother and my brothers Bulis and Dymnos sat down on the scrubby grass, sap-stained and tired after harvesting, and shared a celebratory meal of bread, garlic and the very first oil pressings.

I wanted to finish it quickly. I had arranged to meet Orpheus later, without my father's knowledge, in case he stopped me seeing him. Whose father would forbid his daughter from consorting with a demi-god? Mine. "Too rich for your blood," he had warned me. "If you upset him, we'll all suffer."

But I didn't care. I didn't even recall the weeping pregnant girl who had thrown herself from the cliff. *Please, meal, end now. Let me go. Let me go to Orpheus.*

I felt it before I saw it.

I jumped up, squealing in pain: I thought I had disturbed a bee because the stinging sensation in my ankle was anonymous and sharp. But it was a snake, a little brown snake, and although my brothers chased it with sticks it escaped into a crevice in the stony hillside. Our neighbour Aristaeus abandoned his sheep to rush to my aid. The breath felt as if it was being crushed from my chest like oil from the olives as the shepherd carried me back to the village to find the physician. After that, I recalled little.

You will note, I hope, that I was not dancing for joy in a meadow after my marriage to Orpheus when the snake struck. Nor was Aristaeus the villain whose unwanted sexual attentions made me flee into the path of the snake. He was just a kind old man who tried to save my life. How could legend have portrayed him so cruelly – or set me as Orpheus's bride? The problem with history, with legends, is that the first version that's told tends to stick in the collective mind. There is no point demanding a right of reply.

I'm told I was raving and semi-conscious for days, and nobody expected me to live. My family had even started making preparations for my funeral rites. But I lived. I woke one day to find my mother standing over me in her pale lavender *chiton*, smiling, scented with cooking herbs, clapping her hands together in obvious joy – but I couldn't hear the claps. She spoke. And although I could see her lips moving, I could hear absolutely nothing she said.

I was deaf.

As friends told me later, it was a small price to pay for surviving the snake's venom. Its poison sometimes had that effect, they said. I admit that it was frightening to be a baby again, learning to understand speech anew, but I made my brothers mouth words at me for hours until I was sure I could understand most of what was said to me. I was just glad to be alive.

There was a posy of dried flowers left for me on the steps of our house. I knew it was from Orpheus, although I didn't dare tell my father. I dreamed of meeting him secretly again.

When I was deemed fully fit, my mother let me go out to the *agora* with Metis, with a few coins so I could treat myself to some thyme-scented honeycomb. If she told Metis to keep a special eye on me due to my handicap, I was in no position to hear it. That can make you very suspicious. It's easy to imagine that everyone is concealing things from you when you can't hear.

But we enjoyed ourselves at the *agora* and wandered from

stall to stall, dripping honey down our chins and dresses as we broke off chunks of the honeycomb I had bought.

"Look," said Metis, accompanying her words with an exaggerated pointing gesture. "Orpheus is going to play." As soon as she said it, I could see that she regretted it, and I read her lips shape the words, "I'm sorry."

I would no longer be able to share the communal rapture as Orpheus played his lyre to the crowd. It was a shame, but I reminded myself that I still had my looks and my life, and that Orpheus was still my sweetheart and had proved it with his gift. I watched him in the way you watch someone very familiar to you but who doesn't know you're looking at them, taking in the movement and the detail of his blond hair and his extravagant wrist movement as he plucked at the strings. It was like watching a loved one sleeping.

But my attention began to wander. It had never done that before, not while Orpheus was there.

The crowd appeared to freeze. There was something unnerving about seeing people standing slack-jawed and immobile around a — around a skinny, frizzy-haired youth with thick-bridged nose and more than a few pimples on his chin and forehead. The realization hit me like cold water. I stared, because I had never noticed them before. I was so fascinated and appalled by this imperfection that I stepped forward.

Orpheus was not as wrapped up in his performance as I had thought. As soon as I moved, he looked up. But his fingers continued their silent progress along the strings of his lyre. *Nobody* so much as twitched a muscle during his recitals. I'd swear he was shocked.

And when his eyes met mine, the sky didn't explode in shooting stars. All I felt was embarrassment at being caught staring at his spots. It clearly troubled him, too, because as I backed away, trying to melt back into the oblivious crowd, his eyes kept darting between the lyre and me as if he could not believe what was happening.

He stopped playing. The crowd fragmented, woken,

surprised. "Hey!" he mouthed at me. "Don't go! Come back."

And he got up to come after me, but I ran. I think I was running from reality, not from him. Deafness had freed me from a spell.

I didn't love Orpheus at all. I knew that now.

#

My mother caught my face in both her hands and forced me to look at her.

"Orpheus is here again," she mouthed, agitated. "He asks to see you. Won't you just talk to him?"

It was the third time Orpheus had come to my father's house and sat outside playing his lyre. Between tunes he threw stones at our door and at our goats. My father was furious: but he didn't dare tell the son of a god to clear off, and took out his anger on me with a switch instead. I would ruin the family, he told me. I deserved what I got. He would drag me out to Orpheus and disown me if I didn't appease the boy.

My mother said nothing, but she did block my father from the doorway the next time he tried to shout silent insults at me.

Bulis came running in, gleeful. "Orpheus is lovesick," he said. I missed a few words because he was prancing around, his face turned away from me. "....just sitting there, pining for you."

If it had been anyone else pining outside our door, I would have grabbed up my cloak and given him an audience. But Orpheus...I had seen the pimples, the flaws, the artful self-conscious conceit in his musical gifts, and I was afraid, both of his menacing persistence and the end of my illusion. Without his heart-stopping tunes, he was nothing.

"Tell him to go away," I said. I could feel my voice in my skull but I had no idea if I were whispering or talking loud enough for him to hear. I didn't care.

Metis was outraged by my lack of gratitude. "You're being

pursued by the son of a *god*. The son of a muse."

"I don't care for him," I said.

But Orpheus, I found, wasn't experienced at taking no for an answer.

I was down in the olive groves, collecting broken branches for firewood after an overnight storm when I felt a hand on my shoulder and smelled unfamiliar sweat. When I turned, it wasn't my father.

"Are you following me?" I demanded.

"I didn't mean to frighten you," said Orpheus. "I just wanted to know why you won't see me. What have I done to you?"

I stared into his ordinary face. No, I felt nothing for him, and I missed that heady sensation and longed to recreate it. I couldn't. "I just don't love you any more. I can't even hear your music. Leave me alone."

He still had his lyre. He grabbed it to his chest and for a moment I thought he was going to strike me with it, not play it. But he played. I could see it. He stopped, stared and twanged the strings hard and they blurred with each blow.

"You really don't want me, do you?" He seemed amazed. "Don't I mean anything? Aren't I handsome enough for you?"

It was a stupid moment. I answered. "No. You're not handsome at all."

His face changed. I tightened my grip on a particularly heavy branch, ready to swing it. He *had* frightened me, and he was still frightening me. It was the intent expression on his face, not that of a disappointed suitor, but the fixed stare of someone teetering on the edge of unpredictable anger. When you're deaf, you can't avoid concentrating on people's faces. "I have no idea why you're pursuing me. You could have any girl in the country."

"You walked away. You weren't affected by my music."

"I can't be. I'm deaf."

I was half-expecting him to say that he wanted me because I wouldn't be swept up purely by his music, that I would love him for what he was. But he didn't. "Nobody walks away from me," he said. He suddenly turned and walked a few steps, and then he swung round: if he had been talking as he walked, I wouldn't have known. "Every woman wants me, sooner or later. So will you."

I felt someone brush close to me and I knew why he had decided to walk away at that moment. Aristaeus had come to check that I was all right. Orpheus stared at him and then left: the shepherd stood by me until he was out of sight.

"Be careful of that one," Aristaeus said, taking my arm like a protective grandfather still trying to pretend he had the strength to defend his family. "He's the kind who wants only what he can't have. You won't find it easy to turn down the son of a god."

#

Like I said, you can never trust myth. Or history, come to that, because they're much the same thing: they're written by the victor. After a few weeks Orpheus gave up sitting outside my father's house and lobbing stones. He dominated my life: every thought I had was collared by the dread of him and what he would do, so much so that even when my father dragged me to the door by my hair I would not go outside.

But I had to go on living, and I had work to do. Sooner or later I had to face the village and the gossip. It was my fault this had happened. My father was right.

I walked down to the spring one morning and found a severed ram's head propped on a rock, trailing a stream of dried dark blood, and I knew who had put it there. The dread gripped me again.

Unlike you who never see the true shape of the meat you eat, we were used to seeing animal heads. I don't care for them myself, eyes or not, but my brothers would fight over them at table. But this was not an abandoned delicacy. It was a message: an escalated threat, a more serious one than thrown stones. I looked round. Deaf or not, I would have sensed someone creeping up on me, but there was nobody there. I filled my water-jugs glancing over my shoulder and then almost ran back home, slopping ice-cold water down my robe as I went, breath catching in my throat.

You cannot refuse the son of a god.

I wondered if Aristaeus was going deaf with age.

#

There were a few more rams' heads at the spring in the weeks that followed, and the feeling that someone was a few strides behind me when I went walking without Metis or my brothers for company. They were the only ones who talked to me anymore. It was as if my constant fear was contagious. I had rituals before I could leave the house, checking after every ten steps that there was nobody behind me. My life had stopped for Orpheus as surely as if I could hear his music again but it was not the delightful pause of time that I had once wished would last forever.

I found myself slipping into the silence. I began to wonder what my voice sounded like beyond the vibration in my own head.

It was market day and the smell of charring lamb would have guided me to the *agora* even if I hadn't known every step of the way. I would stop and see if they were selling the tiny shanks smothered in sage and rue. It was a rare treat. When I got to the market, the crowds were unnaturally still.

Of course. Orpheus the maestro, Orpheus the irresistible, was giving one of his carefully-impromptu recitals, one foot on an overturned amphora. Nausea swept over me and my scalp and throat prickled hot with panic. I had to get away. Even with so many people there, he could hurt me: men, women, children and goats stood facing forward as if awaiting a revelation. They would never be able to come to my aid. Grease from those flute-sized shanks spilled down my gown. I backed away and then turned to run.

If I thought I was the only living thing able to move freely while Orpheus played, I was wrong. Two young men were walking towards me. It was all wrong. Orpheus was playing. They should have been frozen. But they started to quicken their pace, staring at me and nobody else.

I didn't recognize them. They could have been from a distant village. But I started to run faster even before I thought about it.

How could they manage to move against the music?

Should I have tried to scream for help? You'd be amazed how hard it is to scream when you're terrified. And who would have heard, or answered, when they were pinned down by the music? I ran. I choked in silence.

I ran through Aristaeus' pastures, but he wasn't there. His sheep and goats scattered: his yellow dog barked and whined and made as if to chase me, but he was a loyal dog, and stayed with his flock. I should have run home. But it was too far, and I was blind with panic, as well as deaf. I ran without a plan, without thought, but I headed for the bay where I thought I would find fishermen mending nets.

Eventually I reached the edge of the cliffs, and I skidded to a halt. The men were jogging after me, almost leisurely, because they must have known I would either collapse or simply have nowhere left to go.

They faced me, smiling. "Come, little one." They held out their arms, blocking both sides of me. "Our master requests your presence. Orpheus commands his chosen one to come to him."

I glanced behind me. I couldn't see the beach, but I knew it was a sheer drop. There was the sea beneath. "No!" I thought I was screaming: perhaps I was mouthing silently like them, too. "No! No!"

"You didn't think Orpheus would let a defective like you snub him, did you?" said the taller of the two. He poked his finger in his ear as if cleaning it, but he pulled out a wad of something straw-coloured, then another wad from his other ear. So that was how they resisted the irresistible, how they managed to walk away from the music.

The shorter one shifted from foot to foot, then lunged forward.

I looked down at the cliff edge. It was a moment of insanity, but I was suddenly an animal, all instinct, no reason. If they took me, there was pain and unending misery ahead. I could stand no more devouring by fear.

I jumped.

#

Death is never as you expect it. If that sounds foolish, remember how detailed my people expect our afterlife to be: we know who we will meet, what they will ask and expect of us, and how we must behave. I still thought the two men were right behind me, even though I was walking in a misty grove and it was so grey and leached of colour that I thought the time was just before dawn.

But I was dead, and I was free of Orpheus and his thugs. For a few moments I was euphoric. And even when the joy began to fade, I started to feel more like the self I had once been.

I was standing on a riverbank. There were ripples on the surface of the water so I knew a small boat was approaching. Its black prow stabbed through the mist and there was a man-shape in it pulling at oversized oars. It drew level with me, and the oarsman heaved the oars inboard. I knew was speaking from the movement of his head, beckoning me, but a hood obscured his face so I couldn't hear him. I did not expect to still be deaf. I thought they sorted that out in the afterlife.

He paused and then flung back the charcoal fabric.

"I said, are you still here? No coin?" His face was loose-skinned and miserable, but he was not the forbidding Charon I expected. Oh, I knew him. I *knew* him. *This* was the ferryman. "No matter. Your beloved is coming for you."

How long had I been here? I fumbled for the wool-felt purse hanging from the belt of my gown, but it was empty.

No coin, no passage across the Styx. Had they buried me? My grieving family owed me two coins for my passage, at the very least, to spare me from limbo.

"What beloved?" I asked.

"Orpheus has charmed Hades himself into letting you back into the land of the living. Isn't that sweet? What a talent that boy has."

My stomach knotted again and went on diminishing until I felt there would be a raw hole visible in me. *No, no, no. Not now. I died. I'm free.* "He's coming here? Aren't I dead?"

"Oh, you're dead. But not for long."

You have a word for this sort of man, I believe, the sort who pursues a woman relentlessly even when she makes it clear that there can never be anything between them. This is the sort of man who will destroy what he cannot have. I didn't plan to die, believe me; but at least I thought it would give me some respite.

Orpheus was coming after me.

I hadn't been dead long enough to begin worrying about what would happen when Orpheus finally died too. You see, all you who find comfort in the idea of an afterlife have never considered who you might be stuck with for all eternity. I was considering it for the first time then, staring at the lugubrious face of a man who could have been a surly uncle.

"I must get away," I said. *I had died for this.* "Orpheus will never take me."

"What are you going to do, kill yourself?" Charon shrugged and slid his oars back in the water. "You might as well wait there. I'll see you again one day, no doubt."

I was left staring into the empty mist drifting on the surface of the Styx. If I'd had a coin or two, I could have crossed and then I could have argued my case with Hades. He wanted to keep his subjects, surely? And wouldn't his sad wife Persephone plead on my behalf, knowing what it was to be a victim of men's whims, to be abducted and raped? It was my only chance. If I could defy a demigod, I could plead with Hades. So I jumped into the water. I didn't care what happened. If it swept me away, so much the better. I wanted to be swept wherever I couldn't be found.

But the water was about knee-deep. I hit the riverbed hard, and scrambled upright, spitting bitter water. Another illusion: another reality that the myth had not prepared me for. Gods were liars too, then, relying on our unquestioning belief to keep us in line. I waded across the Styx, looking behind me every ten steps just as I had when I spent every waking moment and much of my dreams harried by Orpheus.

I stepped from the water and my gown wasn't wet. Where could I escape him now? I hadn't planned to die, but when I realised I had, I was comforted that death would give me respite. And underneath my hunted anxiety I felt a hard tightness for the first time, a knot of anger.

He robbed me of my peace. Now he robs me of death. And the knot grew larger.

The Underworld was crowded like a city, like Athenai but without the sunshine and a sense of purpose. For a moment I wondered how I would find Hades himself: but he found me, or to be exact, Persephone appeared out of a melting crowd of shades to confront me. She was much younger, much prettier than I imagined. We all give gods faces, I suppose.

"There is no escape from Orpheus," she said. "My Lord Hades does not break his word."

"Has he promised Orpheus that he can reclaim me?"

"His music is most persuasive."

"I won't go back. I won't let him have me. You don't know how scared I am. You just don't understand."

"We are women, and gods always get what they want. How many of them were conceived in rape? Do not delude yourself." She leaned forward, all mist-grey elegance and sorrow. "And never tell me again that I don't understand fear. *Never.*"

I was still more terrified of Orpheus than I was of an angry goddess. "You leave Hades for half the year."

Persephone lost her composure for a moment, fumbling with the silver silk tassels on her belt. "My mother froze the earth to force him to release me."

"And she set Hecate to protect you down here. So can you not help me?"

Sometimes women pity sisters in the same predicament, but there are also those who want for some reason to see others suffer their own fate. Perhaps they want to be reassured they could not have avoided their misery. Perhaps they want to share sorrow, or resent those who escape. I did not know what sort of woman Persephone had been.

"If Orpheus looks back at you when he leads you from here, he must leave you here," she said. "Until he dies, of course. That is all I can do for you." She turned and began fading back into the milling shades.

"Ask your Lord Hades how he feels to be duped by a boy with a lyre," I called. The anger that had started as a small knot was now insistent, enveloping, taking over my whole body and closing my throat, dead or not. "Ask him if he wants to be robbed of his citizens by the son of a lesser god."

Persephone paused for a moment, and she looked back at me. Perhaps she wanted me to hear her. It might have been simple surprise.

"I shall," she said.

She had given me all she could. It was up to me to use the information. I walked back to the banks of the Styx and waded across towards a gathering crowd of shades on the far bank, awaiting their passage, coins in hand. And then I saw Orpheus, not a shade but a man among them. He was standing with his back to the river, shifting from foot to foot, agitated, impatient. For a moment, I felt the sick dread I'd known when I saw the rams' heads: and then it was gone, replaced by a surge of anger, of indignation, that made my head buzz.

I was afraid of him, but I was enraged as well. I hated him. It was suddenly more than an emotion: it was the whole of me. And I knew exactly how I would make him look at me and lose me.

"Orpheus," I called. My voice jammed in my throat. "I'm

sorry. Don't hurt me. Don't hurt my family. I'll come."

If he replied I didn't know. He began walking backwards, awkward, glancing to the side of him, and then he must have realized there was no way of seizing me without looking back at me: he tugged at the fabric knotted round his waist as a belt and tied it round his eyes. I wondered if I should run, but Hades would no doubt have returned me to him.

And I no longer wanted to run from the object of my fear. I wanted to tear at it. I hesitated, but I did what I thought I would dread most. I reached out to touch his back-stretched hand.

"This way, Orpheus," I called. "This way." And I walked up to him. Head turned away, he grasped my hand hard and I steeled myself to relax so he would think I was coming willingly and had surrendered to him. As he led me away, he stumbled over roots and rocks, and reached up to pull the cloth from his eyes.

He was so certain I was finally overcome by his persistence and his threats. It seemed not to have occurred to him that my dread might be equally persistent. I flung myself at him, dug my fingers into his face and grabbed his stringy yellow hair. We fell to the ground. He was far stronger than me, but I had his hair and I had my full weight and rage upon him, and all I needed was to hang on long enough to make him look at me. I could see his mouth opening and swearing and screaming. He punched me aside, but I hung on to his hair. Blind anger is a great strength, you see, and even a girl like me can fight with enough fury for fuel: and then, without conscious thought, I sank my teeth hard into his nose like an animal. The taste of salt blood shocked me and I was staring into his horrified, cheated eyes.

No is one of the easiest words to lip-read, by the way. He was mouthing that over and over until the invisible hand that jerked him away threw him back through a circle of brilliant gold light.

Then the horizon was suddenly grey again. I steadied myself and spat the blood from my mouth, feeling suddenly sick with the taste and the passing shock. But he was gone. I was one of the free dead again, and even if this was limbo, even if this was far from the Elysian fields, I had escaped Orpheus this time, and that was heaven enough for me.

I had a while – a long while – to get to know Persephone and Hecate, neither of whom had any reason to side with men or gods. Perhaps we could become sisters, if not friends.

#

Hermes came with a new citizen for Hades a few days ago. Even though it had been a year since I had last seen him, the sight of Orpheus's face resurrected a blind fear, but I was ready for it. He brought the marks of his death with him. He was torn and cut. His neck looked...odd. His lyre was clutched in one hand, by the strings.

Persephone and Hecate watched him without expression as Hermes handed him over to Charon on the far bank.

"More angry women," Hecate repeated, because I had not caught her words the first time. "He claims the women of Thrace were so offended when he rejected their sexual advances that they tore him apart and threw his head into the sea. With his precious lyre, too."

"And I hear that when he came to their village to seduce them with his music and rape them, they drowned out his sound with screaming," said Persephone. "Then they knocked his lyre aside and took a slaughtering knife to him, a warning to all men that women will only tolerate so much, even from the son of a god."

I could not take my eyes from him. When you fear a man to the point of death and then see him again as a creature stripped of power, you feel foolish. I felt guilty again, guilty and stupid and stinging with the memories, but now I didn't feel afraid at all.

But what would happen to him? Would he come after me again?

Persephone gave me a slight smile and steered me in front

of her in that way she had when she didn't want me to miss a word of what was being said. "My Lord Hades hates an upstart," she said. "And he also hates to lose. Come and see where Orpheus will spend all time."

#

These days I spend my time with the Queen of the Underworld and the Queen of the Crossroads, my good sisters, my friends, keeping Hades in his place. No, he was not amused by a boy who used his divine talent to rob him of a citizen who was rightfully his. It took him a little time to devise a suitable punishment for an arrogant musician, but the result was inventive.

I will have to tolerate the myth that says Orpheus was reunited with his beloved Eurydice. In a way, it's true. More or less.

Orpheus sits playing his lyre in a sealed room with only Arachne the deaf weaver for company. Sometimes I stop to look, and then move on. Arachne says she doesn't know what all the fuss is about. The boy has pimples.

Orpheus, plucking at his untuned lyre to an audience of a single uncaring deaf weaver, still prefers to think he was killed because the women of Thrace couldn't take no for an answer. He's the son of a god. Women just don't appreciate undying love.

Well, he would say that. Wouldn't he?

VIEW OF A REMOTE COUNTRY

(First published in *On Spec*, Spring 2004. Another exercise written at Clarion East workshop in 2000.)

The audio tape had been the hardest thing to get, but he'd found it in one of those freak magazines you saw people with green hair and pierced lips buying in Smith's. He'd had to ask one of the weirdoes to point it out the magazine to him, though. The table tennis ball and the red light bulb had been much easier to buy.

It seemed a pretty simple kit for reaching out into the paranormal. Evan cut the ball into two halves with some difficulty. The eggshell plastic was tougher than he'd thought, and he didn't want jagged edges sticking into his eyelids. So he filed down the rim of each hemisphere with one of Annie's emery boards and checked it with his fingertip. Then he put his chair into a reclining position, plumped up the cushions, and made sure the door was locked.

He didn't want Annie walking in on him. It would have meant a lot of explanations. He switched off the room light, flicked on the lamp with the red bulb, and lay down to let the Walkman feed shapeless noise into his ears.

He hesitated before covering his eyes: he must have looked a complete dickhead. But the halves of the ball fitted over his eyes without too much discomfort and he forgot how daft it was.

The non-noise washed over him and his closed eyes couldn't detect even the usual wash of collared flashes. It was emptiness, total and complete nothing.

He could see better now. Much, much better.

#

"It's true, I tell you. You can stick a pin in a map and concentrate on it and you can see the place in your mind."

Evan sat swinging his legs over the edge of the scaffolding, which he knew was a daft thing to do nine stories up, but it helped him think. He ate his packed lunch with the bricklaying gang and with Kev in particular. They didn't mess around. Half an hour's break, and they'd be right back on the job, because they got paid by what they finished during the day. They were an elite, like plasterers. He wanted that sort of respected skill someday. He wanted to be more than a builder's labourer.

"Give over," sneered Kev.

"It's true. The American secret service used it for years. It was on telly at Christmas. On BBC2." If it had been on the BBC, it *had* to be true: Evan was getting annoyed. Why wouldn't people believe him? "It's called remote viewing."

"You're the bleedin' remote one."

"I tell you the Americans spent millions on it because they thought the Russians were using it. They reckon they got results from it, looking inside Russian army bases, but of course they won't talk about it now."

"Well, they wouldn't would they?"

"Are you taking the piss?"

"Yes. 'Bout time you got an apprenticeship an' stopped pissin' around with that twilight zone shite," said Kev.

Evan bristled. "It's not shite, it's science." But Annie said it was shite too, although that wasn't the word she used. And Kev had a recent registration second-hand BMW, so he was a man to be listened to. "You have to train yourself for it."

"How? Pin-holdin' classes?"

"No, you clear your mind by going in to a deeply relaxed state by shutting out outside noise and light."

"How'd you do that?"

Evan was so caught up in the explaining that he didn't even stop to think. "You play white noise on your Walkman and you put two halves of a table tennis ball over your eyes and use a red light in the room. It's like *total sensory deprivation*." He hoped he'd said that right. "You can even do telepathy while you're in it."

Kev looked at him. For a moment Evan thought he was thinking about remote viewing seriously. Then Kev burst out laughing and sprayed bits of egg sandwich from a great height.

"You're off your 'ead," he said. "Table tennis balls. Bollocks, more like."

Lunch was over. Evan grabbed the scaffold rail and pulled himself inboard again, chastened and regretful. He wouldn't mention it again.

But he wished he wasn't the only one on the site who watched documentaries. It was lonely liking clever stuff.

#

Evan hadn't had a great deal of success with the map visioning, but that was because he couldn't find a way of checking what he thought he saw against what was really there. He needed someone to check the places for him. But finding the right person round here was a bit of a problem. On the way home he picked up a large haddock, chips and pea fritter from the takeaway and wandered back to the flat, running the gauntlet of under-tens whose entire range of English seemed to consist of the word *fuck*. It was a relief to get in and put the security chain on the door.

Beyond that point, his world was newly decorated in hint-of-peach emulsion and he could sink into the charcoal velveteen sofa knowing it was clean and that he and Annie had paid for it. It was *remote*. He wished it could be even more remote from this neighbourhood.

Annie was working overtime at the 24-hour supermarket. She wanted to earn as much as possible, she said, because that was the only way out of a council flat. Annie, according to his mum, was "getting above herself": she had started taking her job seriously, thinking about applying to be a supervisor, and she had started losing weight and dressing in sober navy blue suits.

Evan had his worries about it too. Annie didn't have to say that it was Evan's fault they only had a council flat, but he heard the rebuke nonetheless. He should have been earning more. He should have done better at school, and got a better job, but he hadn't. He was a failure. And she was getting slim and pretty. How much longer would she want a loser like him?

Only watching TV gave him any self-respect. Since he'd been working on the building site, telly was about all he had the energy for in the evenings. But he found he *liked* the documentaries aimed at clever people, especially the science ones. Television told him, quietly and privately in his own home, who he really was.

He had the flat to himself. He set up the reclining chair in the front room, swapped the light bulbs and finished his fish and chips watching the six o'clock news. It was like eating your dinner in a submarine at night, all red-lit and unreal. He'd seen that in a documentary too. But it was about the Second World War and he didn't know if modern submarines ever surfaced at night. He'd go and look that up sometime.

The news finished and he listened just long enough to the weather forecast to find out if he'd be working on site tomorrow (partially cloudy and dry, so yes, he would) before squeezing the greasy paper into a tight ball and throwing it in the bin. He paused. Lying at this angle, and looking up out the window, all he could see was treetops against the fading light. The city skyline had disappeared below the level of the windowsill. He could kid himself that he was living in the country.

Walkman, eye-covers, and relax. He was getting better at it now. The day's chatter dissolved into a blood-red nothing. He could hear his own pulse, *whoosh-slap, whoosh-slap, whoosh-slap,* and his breathing was easy and deep, as if he could stop it at any time and not feel uncomfortable. Then the intermittent thoughts quieted.

He floated. He waited.

Pictures and sounds came. He was learning to take hold of them very softly so he didn't crush them. There were voices, one of them Annie's, saying how she wished he'd get a grip and earn proper money. She'd told him that before. It was slightly different this time, very distant. He drifted for ages and then time seemed to stop. He took off his eye-shields and looked at the clock. An hour had gone. He felt fine.

Evan was washing up just before the Channel Four documentary was due to start, savouring the bliss of an evening of doing and watching exactly what he wanted, when he began to wonder about it. When he relaxed in the red light and white noise, what was he sensing? Were they his inner thoughts, or were they really someone else's?

It bothered him that Annie's worries had reached into his private red world.

He needs to start earning real money.

No, that was what her voice had said. *He.* Not you, *he.* She was talking to someone, or thinking about him. He wasn't remembering a conversation.

Jesus, he'd *sensed* something.

It worked.

Evan was so excited he almost missed the start of the evening's documentary. He slid down into the armchair right on the start of the title sequence, but his mind, unusually, was not on the program at all.

#

"Your Annie still working nights?"

"Yeah. Good money."

"Don't you like her or something?"

Evan had started to find the line between keeping embarrassing honesty to himself and yet not lying to Kev. The big bloke knew when he was making things up. Evan shrugged. "I like it better when she's not there going on at me, and besides I can watch anything I want on telly."

Kev grunted approval. "You found that out young."

"I like telly."

Evan spotted the bricks were running low as Kev layered them with an astonishing rhythm: mortar, slap, spread, whump, scrape, mortar, slap, spread, whump, scrape. He tapped the bricks into line with the handle of the trowel with such ease that for a moment Evan thought that the highest aspiration a man could have was to be a master brickie. It was hypnotic. It was like watching a weaver, like he had seen on TV. There was nowhere round here you'd ever see a real live weaver.

It seemed a good time to break the flow of conversation. Evan darted along the flexing scaffold boards and dropped down the ladder to fill the hod with more bricks. That was what he was there for. A brickie's labourer fetched and carried.

"You still on that telepathy thing?" Kev asked, not breaking his rhythm.

"Nah." There, he lied. "Just a laugh."

"Yeah," said Kev, and went on weaving a building.

#

It wasn't that Annie was a nagger. She just wanted the best for him. Evan walked home through the centre of town and pondered on his relationship. Annie was right: he needed to get some skills and take the randomness out of life. Good wages gave you choices, and they both wanted a nice house and some security. If he didn't try catching up with Annie, her ambitions and new figure might take her away from him for ever.

At fourteen, she was all he had wanted. At twenty, he had changed. He still wanted Annie, but he wanted himself, too, and it was a self he hadn't known was there when he fell in love with her at school. He had seen amazing things on the telly and they fired feelings in him that his schoolteachers never had. Why hadn't they told him about planets with air that could crush you flat and pharaohs who took drugs and Mongolian monks who could sing two tunes at once? The telly was a far better teacher, one who never called you a failure and always had all the answers.

He'd looked up the word *television* in the dictionary and found that it meant seeing at a distance. It still gave him a flutter of excitement in his chest to think how far he could see from his two-bedroom flat, all thanks to the telly.

He walked past the library, a glass-fronted building spilling bright light that looked as frightening as an expensive fashion shop. People like him didn't go in there. But he stopped to look at the posters taped to the inside of the glass so passers-by could read them.

Among the photocopied sheets telling him about drop-in centres, ward councillors and benefits advice, there was one that caught his eye.

CROP CIRCLES, DOWSING AND LEY LINES? it read. FICTION OR SCIENCE? THE PSI GROUP MEETS TUESDAYS 8pm AT THE ELDON ARMS.

It gave him a strange excitement in his stomach; he memorized the time and place. Next time Annie was working nights, he might even go to a meeting. It was one of those possibilities.

#

"What are you going to be doing with yourself tonight?" asked Annie. She was pulling on her coat over the top of her

Tesco's uniform, about to go on the late shift. "Is there anything good on TV?"

Evan smiled at her fondly. "I thought I'd go down the Eldon." She looked great now, even in her shop clothes. They'd asked her if she wanted to train as a relief checkout supervisor, and he was fiercely proud of her achievement and frightened of it at the same time. He kept her success from his mum. "I haven't been down the pub in ages."

"Well, you enjoy yourself. You ought to, after all that overtime lately."

"I will," he said. It was only a little lie, the pub. It wasn't really a lie at all.

Walking into the Eldon and going up to the Psi Group took every scrap of courage he had. There was a point at which he would rather have picked a fight with someone twice his size than ask someone if he'd come to the right table for crop circles. But he knew he had.

The table was covered in pint pots of murky-looking beer and even the women in the group were saying they'd have a half of Horndean Special Bitter or 6X, and he knew that was real ale.

"I'm Evan," he said.

A beer-drinking woman looked up. "Hi Evan! Glad you could come." The friendliness swept over him like a tidal wave, and he wasn't prepared for it. "What's your special interest, then? Ley lines?"

I'm home, he thought. The far-away place of exciting ideas was right here. "Remote viewing," he said.

"Heavy stuff," said one of the men.

They sat and talked and shared weird experiences and discussed theories. They drank. (And the real ale was another world, too, a lifetime away from his usual lager. This was what students drank, people with an education.) They asked him about remote viewing and he told them how he'd done the mind-clearing telepathy technique with the red light and white noise before trying the stuff with the maps.

Nobody laughed.

In fact, they wanted to know more. Someone called Mick who was studying engineering said he might try that before dowsing next time, and did he have any recommendations about tapes to play? They all talked and talked, and by the time the barman started collecting the glasses and making pointed remarks about having homes to go to, Evan had been invited on a dowsing day and agreed to swap information with at least two other people who said they'd love to work on the remote viewing with him.

He wandered home in ecstasy. It took him ages to drop off to sleep. *Clever people* took him seriously. He found himself giggling like a kid in the darkness.

#

Evan touched the Ordnance Survey map of the Marlborough area spread out on his kitchen table, just where Mick the student had guided his hand. He shut his eyes.

"What can you see?"

"Er … no trees." The image was up to the left for some reason, or at least he felt his eyes were trying to turn that way. "Just grass. Stones."

There was a pause. "Go on."

"Big shapes." Evan waited a little longer and then opened his eyes. Mick was one of the Psi Group people who'd offered to help out on viewing. They'd been dowsing together the previous weekend. "What was the point on the map, then?"

"Avebury."

"Oh."

"I think that's pretty good."

"Why?"

"You don't know Avebury, do you?"

"No. What is it?"

"It's like Stonehenge. Lots of standing stones."

Evan hoped for a moment that he had seen clearly, just as he thought he had heard Annie in his red and white trance a few months ago. "I could have sort of picked that up without realizing it and seen the map and just guessed lucky."

"We can test it." Mick folded the map up and looked at his watch. Like Evan, he knew Annie was back just after ten every night this week and they had an agreement not to mention the funny stuff in front of her. Just beer. "You know, that's a good attitude in investigation."

"What is?"

"Scepticism. Thinking that there might be a more mundane explanation."

He was comfortable with words like mundane now. "How can we test it?"

"We could find a different map of somewhere that I can see or get pictures of and that you couldn't know about. Like the inside of a building."

"Okay. Want to do that Monday? Annie's back on nights."

"Fine." Mick drained his cup of coffee and put the map in his pocket. It was battered, and folded on top of folds, probably from all those crop circle trips. "Has it ever worked for you, that meditation business? The white noise?"

"Sort of. Well, yes." It was one thing to describe a stone circle, and another to admit you thought you'd heard your girlfriend telling someone you were a useless tosser. Or he might have guessed that as well. "I was sure I'd heard my girlfriend talking about me or thinking about me."

"Something you could have created from what you already knew?"

Evan nodded sadly. "I'll try it again. Now that I'm getting in the swing of this."

"See you Monday then."

"Yeah. See you."

Evan wiped up the cups and put them away in the cupboard over the sink. The red bulb was still in the table lamp. He had about twenty minutes until Annie was due in, so he went back into the living room and put the armchair in the recline position. He laid back and plugged in, eyes covered, for one last try tonight because he was in the right mood.

Quiet came. He had a brief glimpse of a holiday in Dawlish as a kid, up in the left of his field of view. The picture had a fuzzy black border. Then he thought of Annie, getting into her J-registration Ford Fiesta, brown leather flying jacket over her uniform. But it didn't look like Tesco's car park at all. And there was someone with her, a bloke, but he was pretty formless. Just a bloke. They drove off. The image went away and Evan waited, but it was the last thing he could concentrate on. He unplugged and replaced the red bulb with a soothing 40 watt light.

"Hello, sweetheart," Annie said, and put her handbag and car keys on the kitchen table. "Miss me?"

"Yes." He had a cup of tea ready for her. "Mick came round for a drink."

"Had anything to eat? I got a takeaway. Chicken korma."

"Bit late for me." He had to ask. He just had to. "Give someone a lift tonight, did you?"

He wished he'd been ready for the reaction, but he hadn't really thought he'd seen a real event. It was just a random thought. It was only a casual question. But she froze. And then he could see it in her lovely face, all of it.

"Yes, I dropped the bakery manager off on the way back, that's all," she said. Her lips were pressed into a line. "Why are you asking?"

Evan's gut shivered. The problem was that he didn't know why — because he had seen something? Because she might have confirmed a suspicion he hadn't even had an hour ago? Or because she might have been carrying on with a man who was a *manager*, someone with a real, serious job?

"I thought you were a bit later than usual, that's all," he said.

Lies. Suddenly his new skill — if that was what it was — seemed to have lost a little of its joy.

#

They didn't discuss the bakery manager next day, or even the day after that. Mick came round as promised on Monday at 6.00pm with a large scale map of the centre of town. Evan told him about the vision — well, he didn't have a better word — of the unidentified car park.

"Jesus," said Mick. "That's interesting."

"But I might have had a subconscious suspicion that she was seeing someone. She's a looker. She could get a better bloke."

"And you have the, um, vision on the night she gives him a lift?"

"She said it was just that. A lift."

"I didn't mean to suggest it wasn't."

Was he that upset about it? Yes. He worried that he was still a brickie's labourer at 20, working in an industry where bad weather put you out of work, and where arthritis or worse made you old at 40. What sort of prospect was he for a woman who wanted a house of her own? At that moment he envied Mick more than he envied the first man on the Moon. Mick had a future of possibilities that went a long way beyond finding interesting books in the library. Mick had an education.

That was the most remote view he had ever seen. It was so far away that it seemed further than space.

"Come on." Mick unfolded a large-scale map of the city and Evan settled himself at the kitchen table with the map spread out before him. He shut his eyes and put his finger in the middle of it. Then he breathed slowly and deliberately. The picture was up on the left again, not at all like looking at TV. It never filled his whole view.

"What can you see?"

"A room, light collared walls, big cupboards and a big window all along one side." He paused. *Whoosh-slap, whoosh-slap, whoosh-slap.* His heartbeat interrupted him. "A white board on the wall with writing on it. Desks. Well, sort of. Rows of tables with metal chairs" He stopped. Annie's potential infidelity interrupted his thoughts. "Nah, that's it.

Sorry."

"Want to know what you've just described?"

"What?"

"The lecture theatre in D Block."

So what? He'd worked on sites all over town. Half the buildings in the city seemed to belong to the university, and he'd seen inside so many of them that he was sure they all looked the same. It was just memories that his brain was churning up like a cement mixer. "Lucky guess," Evan said.

"You always doubt yourself. Whatever you see, you explain it away."

"I think I'm being bloody silly."

Mick gave him an impatient look and shook his head. "Come on. Shut your eyes and let's have another go." He obeyed. The map crackled as Mick picked it up and repositioned it, and he felt the draught of its movement on his face.

"Do you ever get the feeling you've done the wrong thing?" Evan asked.

"All the time," said Mick.

"I mean that you've missed out on something."

"Anything in particular?"

"School." He opened his eyes. "Education."

Mick looked at Evan for a long time, and that made him feel uncomfortable, because the blokes on the building site never did that unless they were picking a fight.

"I always got the feeling you weren't a bricklayer at heart," Mick said.

"I'm not even a bricklayer. They've got a real craft. I'm just a brickie's labourer."

Mick shuffled his feet and leaned back in the chair, fiddling with the plastic tie from a six-pack.

"Don't have to stay one, do you?"

"I didn't get my exams," Evan said.

"You still can."

"I'm not going back to classes. Not book stuff, anyway. If I couldn't do it then, I can't do it now."

"That's crap. You can learn to do anything if you want to. What are you afraid of? That your girlfriend and your mates won't know you any more?"

It was closer to the truth than he wanted to admit. Changing who you were was hard on everyone. He didn't really like the idea of Annie losing weight, even if she did look really good now, just in case she left him. He thought the car park vision was just his worst fears breaking loose in his mind.

"I'm not afraid," he lied. "I'd just feel an idiot sitting in a classroom at my age."

"People learn to program computers in their 80s. Think about it."

After Mick left, he settled on the sofa and watched the football. He turned the sound down. The match was pretty poor and he didn't care much about the Italian league. He wanted to see something interesting, like the volcano that could blow up and wipe out Naples at any time, the one he'd seen on the documentary last week. That'd ruin their game. A hole in the ground that could wipe out a city. It was amazing.

He thought about classes. What would Annie say? How much would it cost them, now they were on one wage most of the time? Even if he did it, how many more exams would he have to take to reach Mick's position, where you had all the possibilities in the world?

Everything seemed so far away right then. It was a long way to see.

#

"I'm lost," Mick said.

They stopped the car. Evan pulled out the sketch map someone had drawn for them and checked it. Taunton that way, turn right at the junction for Glastonbury. Mick had said a trip to Glastonbury would be a laugh, because everyone there believed in ley lines and dowsing. It was the local industry. He'd even promised Evan a walk up the Tor.

Evan inspected the hand-drawn map. "Looks like we're not at the junction yet," he said. Whoever had drawn it hadn't put in useful things like pubs and road numbers, and he'd never been to Somerset, so it was all guessing. "I suppose we just carry on and look for signs to Taunton."

"Okay. If we see a garage first, I'm getting a proper road atlas." Mick pulled out of the lay-by and they travelled in silence. The throb of the car stereo was soothing even though it was loud.

"Have you done anything about evening classes?" Mick asked.

"Not yet."

"Discussed it with Annie?"

"No."

The music covered the silence between them. He saw a landscape in his mind, just there, up on the left again, for no reason.

"You'll come to a white building with a yew tree in front soon," he said. *Where did that come from?* "Hundred yards on the right, there's a pub with a painted sign with a horse on it and then the turning is on your next right."

"Ok-ay," Mick said, slowly.

The car drove on and they came to white building with a yew tree in front. A hundred yards on there was a pub with a painted sign showing a Grey horse. Mick slowed down and pulled up to stare at it: a couple of cars swerved round them, one honking in fury.

"I don't think we need the atlas," said Mick. He looked a little shaken, all white and quiet. "Very impressive."

"I did it, didn't I?"

"Yes. You did."

And suddenly Evan knew what the Tor would look like, and what he would be able to see from its summit, the whole county spread out around him like a giant map. He could do it. He could do something he had *learned* to do. He could do something the CIA trained really clever people to do, and if he could do that, he could learn to do *anything*. But if it was a fluke, a crazy piece of luck – no, he slapped down the doubt that was already creeping up on him. *No*. He wouldn't let that voice whisper *failure, failure* at him any longer.

He had a future that telly couldn't show him. It was unknown because it was for him to shape, and he would start shaping it in small ways by going back to class.

He thought he might have whooped out loud, but instead he sank into silence. He saved the whoop of joy for the moment he stopped at the top of Glastonbury Tor, out of breath and elated, and turned to see the map-landscape of green and gold and copper exactly as he expected.

Evan knew for sure that the road to the remote country was close – close enough to touch.

THE MAN WHO DID NOTHING

(First published in *Realms of Fantasy,* June 2003. Year's Best Fantasy & Horror #17. Also Honourable mention, Year's Best Science Fiction #21)

Hursley Rise, May 2

There was a boy – five, maybe six – sitting on half a discarded mattress by the kerb as Jeff drove down the road. At first he thought the child was trying to open a bottle of pop, but the closer he got, the better he could see that the boy was making a petrol bomb.

Jeff slowed to a crawl and then stopped. He didn't dare switch the engine off, not here. A daffodil nodded in the grass at the side of the road and the whine of a power-drill competed intermittently with music throbbing from an open window. The normality didn't reassure him; he opened the car window about six inches.

The child was trying to thread some rags into the neck of a beer bottle, pausing every so often to hold the bottle up to the light, sigh, and resume his task of working the rag into the neck of the bottle with his index finger.

For a moment Jeff thought about getting out and taking the thing from him. Then an older boy in the latest Manchester United tracksuit walked up to the kid and crouched over him, like a protective elder brother, and took the bottle gently from him. He examined the wick, pushed it further into the bottle and handed it back to the kid.

That was how you did it. Then both boys looked up at Jeff, as if moving as one.

"Antichrist! Fuckin' antichrist!" they shouted. And the bottle – unlit, mercifully – arced and crashed onto the road just short of the driver's door. Both boys ran back up the road, not looking back.

He could have – *should have* – got out of the car and taken the lethal little toy from the kid. He should have marched him back to his own front door and berated his mother for letting such a tiny child handle potential destruction. He should have done something.

But he didn't. It was Hursley Rise, and these were dangerous times, and the shabby little housing estate was going mad. He accelerated away towards the city centre.

#

Hursley Rise citizens' drop-in centre, nine days earlier.

"I don't see why he should be living next door to me," said the woman in the interview booth. She smelled of chip fat and Issey Miyake perfume: in the small plaster-boarded space the combination was distracting. "He's the Antichrist. Can't you do something about it? Get him moved or something?"

It wasn't an unusual request to make of your ward councillor. Since Jeff Blake had started holding evening surgeries at the community centre, he had seen two constituents complaining about military radar upsetting their racing pigeons, and a man who had lined his loft with cooking foil to stop military intelligence beaming messages into his home. He had wanted an improvement grant to pay for lead sheet, just to be on the safe side.

"How do you know he's the Antichrist, Mrs Avery?" Jeff asked. He caught the inside of his cheek discreetly between his teeth to stifle a laugh. You couldn't mock a voter a week before an election. "I mean, we can't just go in and evict the bloke like that. The courts will want some grounds for action."

"He's evil. Pure evil."

"Well, lots of people aren't very loveable, Mrs Avery. It doesn't make them the devil."

"Since he moved in there's been nothing but trouble in our road. He's a weird old sod. Lives on his own. The kids are terrified of him."

"Yes, but why do you think he's the Antichrist?" She looked at him for a brief blank moment, as if the word had thrown her. Then she puffed a sigh and began rummaging in her bag. While her head was tilted down, he could see the darker roots in her red spiky hair. A packet of low-tar cigarettes and the latest, tiniest, slimmest mobile phone clattered onto the melamine table while she excavated.

"There," she said at last. And she handed him a creased strip of newspaper.

The headline was from one of the tabloids: ANTICHRIST WILL APPEAR ON COUNCIL ESTATE, WARNS RECLUSE. The story reported the ramblings of a man who predicted the new millennium would see the arrival of the Beast in a humble home. The man, said the story, had no electricity, phone or mains water but kept track of world events by communing with the cosmic consciousness on his allotment. He claimed the Antichrist would be identified by the trail of havoc he left behind him.

Jeff handed the cutting back to Mrs Avery. "I thought it was six-six-six," he said.

"What is?"

"The identifying mark of Satan."

Mrs Avery scowled. She had one of those flat, hard little faces with thin lips and broad noses, the prevailing type on the estate. Inbred, he decided, whining and helpless: it wasn't a view he would voice, not even to his wife Bev. He wished secretly for the working class of his dad's generation, skilled manual workers with scrubbed front doorsteps, all neat proud poverty and a horror of hire purchase.

"You'll laugh the other side of your bleedin' face when he starts," she said. She stood and slung her bag over her shoulder. "And don't expect me to vote for you, neither. I'm coming back with a petition."

Hers was just one vote. He had a seven thousand majority here, even if the party was holding on to overall control of the council by just one seat. And, as leader, he was assured a safe one. He watched her departing back with no regrets. "Silly cow," he said to himself.

He gathered up his papers to go home. He was on time. He wouldn't have to grab a takeaway as a peace offering to a huffy Bev, silently angry after yet another dinner left to congeal in the oven on a low heat.

While he was fumbling in his briefcase for his car keys, his phone warbled. He put the case on the roof of the car and took the phone – clunkier, older, less desirable than mad Mrs Avery's chic device – from his jacket.

"Jeff Blake."

"Jeff, it's Warren. We've got a bit of a problem."

"Christ, when haven't we?" He could hear bar sounds in the background. "Are you in the staff club?"

"Yeah."

"I thought you were supposed to be out canvassing for Graham. Some poxy deputy you are – "

"Well, this is about Graham." Rustling noises and a sudden drop in the background noise suggested Warren had moved somewhere secluded. "He's in a spot of trouble."

"What now? Drink driving?"

"Computer porn. Accessed using the council network."

"Who knows about it?"

"Only a few people. IT staff, internal audit and the chief executive."

"Okay, first thing in the morning, I want you and him in my office. First thing, mind. I want it sorted."

Jeff got in the car and sat for a few minutes in despairing silence before turning the key and moving off. A slithering noise above his head followed by a dull thud made him hit the brakes. He looked in the rear view mirror: his briefcase, split open by the fall from the car roof, was scattering papers to the breeze.

"Oh, bollocks," he said. And Mrs Avery's Antichrist seemed like an easier problem to deal with right then.

#

Memo
To: Head of Housing Service
From: Hursley Area Housing Manager
Re: 15 Barton Crescent
We have had six more complaints from tenants today asking us to evict Michael Warburton of 15 Barton Crescent on the basis that he is the antichrist. We have also had a similar complaint from an owner-occupier in Waverley Gardens about Frank James Morton of Flat 35. My staff have explained we have no power to evict if there is no breach of the tenancy agreement, and that they can't both be the Antichrist. I know these people have unusual views but we are aware there is talk of "doing the job" themselves. I would appreciate some support and advice on the situation before it boils over.

#

There was a Victorian oil painting of a former lord mayor hanging in the corridor leading to Jeff's office at the town hall. It always bothered him. As he walked closer, he could see a grotesque, round-faced figure with cartoon-like circular eyes, and as he drew level with it the face resolved into grim patriarchal realism. He knew it was just the light playing on the swirls and textures of the oil paint. But these days all things seemed sinister, imbued with darker meaning.

Graham Vance was already sitting in the office looking for all the world like a schoolboy in need of a good slap. His face seemed as if the years had been put on it by a make-up artist, creped and puffed and greyed on top of youth, as if he could be restored to his boyish prettiness by just peeling it all off.

Go on, cower, you little shit, Jeff thought. *I'll teach you to risk this party's majority.* He leaned forward and braced his elbows on his desk.

"Why the hell did you do this through the council network? You know it's monitored."

Graham shrugged. "So what have I done?"

"Downloading child porn."

"No way."

"You've e-mailed pictures to all your noncey mates, too. Don't lie to me."

Vance looked slightly thrown. He pulled a dismissive face. "It's a private matter. And it was just pictures, only teenagers. It's not as if I've been caught with a little kid, is it?"

"I don't believe what I'm hearing. You make me sick."

"Prove I've done something illegal."

"Someone probably could, but what worries me most is what it looks like to the voters." Jeff glanced down the printout on his desk: line after line, thousands of them, of www's and .coms and incomprehensible things – except for words like *ripe schoolgirls* and *Toilet Boy*. "You're on one of the social services sub-committees. What are you going to do?"

"Do I have to do anything?"

"I'd suggest you resign but it's too close to the election and we'd have to explain you away to the media."

Graham didn't appear contrite. "Fuss about bugger all, really."

"Really? Like the drink-driving, and the prostitute on the civic trip to France?"

"It's pretty harmless stuff. Nothing extreme."

"I wouldn't know, and I'm not much inclined to look at it,

either. That's Audit's job. You're a disaster waiting to happen for this party." Jeff gave up trying to stare him into an apology and leaned back in his chair. "After the election, if we get back in – if you get back in – "

"You need my seat to keep overall control of this council," Graham said. "You want the opposition to walk in? This is dirty washing we can do in private." He paused. "You can talk the chief exec out of taking this to the Standards Committee, can't you?"

"Can't promise," Jeff said, hearing himself bluff and hating himself for it. "Now piss off and don't let me hear another word out of you."

He sat alone in his office with the door shut for a long time after Graham had left, and tried to clear his correspondence. So men looked at porn on the net: it was human nature. With any luck, Graham might not have done anything criminal. He'd see the chief internal auditor later, just to make sure he knew the size of the problem.

But it was time he should have been out canvassing. One-seat majorities didn't look after themselves.

#

PETITION
From the Residents Action Committee of Hursley Rise
To Dennington Vale Borough Council
We the undersigned want the Antichrist and his accomplices off of our estate so decent people can live in peace and safety. We know who they are and where they are. We have a list of them. They should not be living near families. If the council don't get them out then we will.

#

The phone rang.

"Answer the bloody thing," Bev growled into her pillow, and pulled the duvet up over her head. Jeff looked at the alarm clock: it wasn't quite midnight. The voice on the end of the phone was a reporter from the local paper.

"Have you got any comment on the riots, Councillor Blake?"

At first the words didn't register. Jeff turned the word *riot* round in his mind. "What riot?"

"I thought you'd know about it by now. They're setting fire to houses at Hursley Rise and there's a running battle between police and residents. About a hundred and twenty coppers there now."

Jeff found himself drowning in panic. *Porn scandal, breakdown of law and order, media circus, election disaster.* "I'll get back to you," he said, and slammed the phone down.

He was into his clothes and halfway down the path to the garage when he remembered he had left without telling Bev where he was going, or even knowing which road he was heading for.

But as he drove closer to Hursley he couldn't miss the glow of a blaze outlining the youth activities centre, or the police vans heading away from it with their blue lights strobing. The last one to pass him bore the livery of the neighbouring county's force: they must have called for reinforcements. A klaxon behind him made him pull over, and a fire engine sped past him, clipping the bollard in the centre of the road.

Even two streets away he could hear dogs barking, glass smashing, occasional cheers. It sounded like a football match. And then he could smell it – petrol, smoke, and diesel exhaust. He rounded the corner by the eight-till-late, where two men were hammering boards across a shattered window, and slowed to a creep.

A dull thud on the back window made him brake hard. The car stalled. He swung round in his seat, expecting a mob and missiles, but there was nothing. Then someone rapped hard on the passenger side window.

"Jesus –"

"Jeff, turn round. Are you bloody insane?" It was Gwen Hillier, another of the three Hursley Rise ward councillors.

He wound down the window. She was pointing frantically, like a crazed race marshal. "I said turn round. Park down Stanley Street."

It took Gwen a few minutes to catch up with him. She leaned on her stick and struggled for breath. The dim red glow shone off the rims of her spectacles.

"I've lived here sixty years and I've never seen them go off like this," she said. "Not that you'd know that, living in Vale End. I've had to run for it. Me! They went berserk and started pointing and saying it was the council's fault for moving them in."

"Who's them? The hordes of Satan?"

"Don't joke. Get round to Barton Crescent and take a look. They won't recognize you, will they? You never come here."

I am the Leader of the Council, Jeff thought. *They'll expect me to do something statesmanlike.* He set off at a jog towards the centre of the estate, slowing sooner than he expected to a wheezing half-walk, half-stumble: middle-age wasn't treating him as well as he had imagined. And then, when he reached the junction of Barton Crescent and the main road through the estate, he saw a scene straight from Hieronymus Bosch.

A small van was lying on its side, ablaze. A fire crew was playing a hose on it, retreating every few seconds under a hail of bricks and bottles from a group of youths. Behind them, another crew was trying to get into a house where flames were spitting from a ground-floor window. A cordon of police with visors and riot shields were forcing back screaming residents to clear a path. Everywhere Jeff looked, there were ugly little cameos of violence and destruction, and a disturbing number of small children picking up debris where it fell and hurling it back into the melee.

And there were TV cameras. Jeff spotted them just after they spotted him. A cameraman and a reporter sprinted across to him, dodging bottles.

"Councillor Blake, what do you make of this?"

Jeff couldn't see past the brilliant white light perched on

top of the camera, and all he could think of was how scruffy he must have looked without a collar and tie.

"It's – it's an outrage," he said. The autopilot that drove all politicians took over. "This is the work of a few hotheads, probably not even locals."

"But what do you say to people who claim you've allowed the Antichrist to move on to an estate full of families and have ignored pleas to move him out?"

"I say it's complete garbage in this day and age. This isn't the middle ages. It's just an excuse for drunken vandalism and I can promise a full enquiry."

The light snapped off, leaving him blinking at yellow after-images, and he was alone again in a sea of chaos.

He paused for a second and felt helpless. An inner voice said *do something*, but nothing practical came to mind. A brick shattered into fragments a few feet from him and he snapped out of the stupor and made a dash for the car.

He'd never seen anything like it. There would be hell to pay in the morning.

The police superintendent walked towards him, flanked by two sergeants. She wiped her brow on the back of one hand, checker-braided cap in the other. "Glad I caught you," she said. "The place has gone mad. Where's all this antichrist stuff come from?"

"Bloody media," Jeff said. "Bloody media."

#

News headlines Wednesday April 25
Fifty arrested in Hursley Rise "Antichrist" riots
Twenty police treated in hospital
Two homes looted and burned after residents flee
Tenants action group threatens to picket town hall to get "devil men" evicted.

#

There was a Japanese film crew waiting on the steps up to the town hall's grand Palladian portico. Jeff watched them for a few minutes from the window of the conference room.

"Look at them all," said the chief executive. "They've set up satellite links at the back of the building too."

"Can't complain we're not on the map now, can we, Lennie?" Jeff sat down and leafed through a pile of morning papers, most bearing some headline with the words *riot* and *Antichrist* in 72 point type. "Welcome to Dennington, City of Nutters."

"He's late," the chief executive said. "Bet he's stopped off to survey the damage."

"Beelzebub?"

"No, Head of Housing."

"Have you spoken to Audit about the stuff Graham Vance was downloading?"

"Yes."

"And?"

"It's pretty serious. Might be a good idea if he stood down from the Social Services sub-committee. And Audit thinks we should call in the police."

"Oh, *that* bad."

"Up to you, of course, Leader."

You could have made that decision yourself, Jeff thought. But it took a singularly brave chief executive to dump his political masters in the mire days before an election, and Lennie McAndrew was not that man. Nor was Graham Vance's taste in pornography the most pressing problem now.

The meeting was more bewildered than grim. While they discussed the cost of repairs and loopholes in tenancy conditions, nobody seemed keen to say a particular word. But Jeff felt he had to.

"How do we deal with the Antichrist angle?"

"Just make a statement that we'll seek eviction of the rioters and that antisocial behaviour won't be tolerated," said Lennie. "Dismiss it as mass hysteria."

Jeff looked at the Head of Housing. He shrugged.

"They're threatening to do the bloke in Stanley Street now."

"Ah, wrong Antichrist, eh?"

"Look, sir, I'm just reporting back. They want us to move him out. They're threatening to march on the town hall tomorrow. We could suggest he move out voluntarily, for his own safety."

"But he doesn't have to go."

"No. He doesn't have to do anything."

"Nothing we can evict him for? Arrears?"

"He's done absolutely nothing, other than being the victim of someone pointing the finger."

Nobody moved. Jeff looked round the table.

"Time for a reassuring visit," Jeff said. "Maybe Superintendent Davis would like to walk round Hursley Rise with me tomorrow. Before the worried citizens of the Rise give the media some handy photo opportunities on our doorstep." He gathered up his papers and headed for his office.

In the corridor, he ran into the chief internal auditor. The only thing he knew about her was that she liked to follow regulations. He always found it odd that a department whose name suggested number-crunching was actually an internal police force.

"Want to see me?" Jeff said.

"Just wondered if you had been made aware of the seriousness of the material Councillor Vance was accessing."

"I gather it's nasty."

"We really need to let the police take a look at the downloaded files. You *are* going to let me refer it to them, aren't you?"

"As soon as I've got the Hursley Rise situation sorted," he promised, and he knew as soon as the words escaped him that he would find a reason not to.

#

Had it not been for a dozen TV news crews, a heavy police

presence and scorch marks around the charred window frames of two boarded-up homes, Hursley Rise looked like any other working-class housing estate that morning. A bull terrier with a lavish studded collar was worrying a black plastic sack of rubbish left on the pavement. A man was up a ladder, painting his upstairs window frames a particularly vivid yellow. A workman was installing a satellite dish on the roof of the Duke of Buckingham pub.

"House-proud area, in parts," said Superintendent Davis. She kept a definite distance from Jeff in the back seat of the police car. He could smell leather, spray starch and the same Chanel scent that Bev wore. "Half the people here are ex-tenants who've bought their homes. Bet their property prices have fallen a bit overnight, eh?"

The patrol car kept up a reasonable pace, slow enough for the two passengers to observe, but too fast to be a target for bricks. Near the row of shops by the bus stop, two constables were engaged in a conversation with a woman pushing a pram.

St Peter and Paul was a redbrick church with a half-hearted bell tower and a peeling notice-board: if the forces of darkness were gathering here, it didn't look like God had his troops on the ground. On the threadbare church green stood around a hundred women and a few men, most accompanied by children of varying ages who were showing signs of boredom. Most had placards, held down like lances so that Jeff couldn't read the words, and two small boys were having a sword-fight with theirs.

"I can talk them out of this," Jeff said. Let me out here and I'll go and meet them."

Superintendent Davis looked unimpressed. "Wouldn't you like me there too?"

"Uniform might start them off again."

He thought he heard her stifle a snort, but he said nothing and stepped out of the car into a chilly morning breeze. The twenty yards to the green suddenly seemed like a very long walk. He glanced back over his shoulder to check where the police car had parked.

As he got closer, some of the crowd turned to stare. A child with a placard was facing him, and he could pick out the words on her white tee-shirt: KILL EVIL NOW. And suddenly he recognized the woman beside her, with her bright red, dark-rooted hair and festoon of gold chain necklaces.

"Mrs Avery," he said. "Are you the – leader of the deputation?"

She narrowed her eyes. There was a cigarette smouldering in her hand, held well away from her own child so that the smoke wafted towards someone else's.

"You come to talk to us now, have you?"

"If that's what you want." He was aware of people closing up behind him. Women and children or not, it was a neck-prickling sensation. "What can I say to reassure you?"

"Just get that bastard out. Or we'll be doing protest marches round the city until you do."

"You know I can't negotiate as long as there's the threat of violence."

Mrs Avery flicked the growing ash from her stub. "Can't blame people if they get frustrated. We told you them blokes was evil."

"You don't really believe there's an Antichrist, do you?"

She stepped a little closer. She was a head shorter than him and none the less terrifying for it. "You go and see him. It's the one next door to me. Stanley Street. The others was just his servants."

Jeff was going to suggest they invite the vicar to join the group to discuss the whole Antichrist concept when a thought hit him, a politician's thought. "Okay, Mrs Avery," he said. "Do you know what I'm going to do now?"

"Amaze me."

"I'm going to walk down to Stanley Street and knock on his door and talk to..."

"Mr Hobbs.

" . . .talk to Mr Hobbs and show you he's just a lonely old

man. A mortal human. And maybe the kids are scared of him because he shouts at them when they're playing too near his garden. Doesn't that sound like a more rational explanation?"

Mrs Avery had a half-smile on her face as she ground her cigarette out under a very high heel. She reached for her daughter's hand and pulled the child to her side. "Come on, Kayleigh, pick your placard up and keep behind the man." She gestured like a commissionaire at a posh hotel. "After you, Councillor Blake."

The worst that could happen, Jeff thought, was that the old boy would come out and threaten them with a walking stick. Then he could slip in and offer him a move to a nice new flat in the city centre, with resident staff and a communal lounge area, and perhaps a cash incentive to help him settle in. He kept walking, aware that Mrs Avery was still behind him but at a growing distance. As they came into Stanley Street, she called out, "Number 27."

The two houses either side were relatively well-kept, one with window boxes of geraniums and one with a red and blue decorative cartwheel hanging on the front wall. But the grass in the gardens was blackened and shrivelled along a foot-wide strip where it flanked the house in the middle.

Between them was a house that appeared not to be part of the street.

Jeff looked again. He looked up at the guttering and the line of the roof, and they ran smoothly into the next property. And yet it did not look *there*.

He put his hand on the gate. The wrought iron was polished, unrusted. The path to the door was immaculately-laid crazy paving, and there were no plants of any kind, not even the odd weed, just bare earth. He put up his hand to knock on the spotless battleship-grey paintwork.

The door swung open. A man in his late sixties stood there, ordinary as could be in grey corduroy trousers and a grey cardigan, smiling. He seemed to like grey a lot. It was then that Jeff felt the rush of cold air past him, as if he had opened a freezer door.

He looked round to say, "See, Mrs Avery, he's just..." but she was too far away. A small crowd standing at stone-throwing distance was staring at the house, and they let loose a volley of bricks. One bounced off the window and hit Jeff in the leg before the old man grabbed his arm and pulled him into the hall to safety.

"You're Mr Hobbs," he said. His leg stung. He glanced down at his trousers, baffled, and then realized the window was probably toughened double-glazing. "Lucky that didn't smash your window."

"No danger of that. I thought you might pop round, Councillor," said Hobbs. "Come and sit down."

The antichrist's front parlour contained two grey velveteen chairs, a television and a plain pine sideboard. There were no photographs on the mantelpiece over the gas fire and no ornaments, except a carriage clock showing 10.23. Above it on the wall where most people might have hung a mirror was a framed sampler, embroidered as usual with an uplifting quotation; *All that is necessary for evil to triumph is that good men do nothing.*

Hobbs appeared in seconds with a tray bearing a pot and two porcelain cups of coffee. It smelled wonderful.

"Can't bear mugs," the old man said. "Got to have a drink out of a proper cup, eh, Councillor Blake?"

"Thank you." The coffee scalded his lips. "I imagine things have been quite hard for you this last few weeks."

"Oh, the stones never touch the house. Don't worry about me."

"Forgive me." Hobbs seemed a pleasant old gent. "They think you're the Antichrist. Wouldn't you like to move out for a while for your own safety? We can get you straight into a new flat. And we'd pay all your expenses, of course."

Hobbs sipped his coffee as if considering the offer. His face was unlined, and his eyes were clear, but all the same he still looked old. "I like it here," he said at last. "I don't have to move, do I?"

"We can't make you, Mr Hobbs. You've done nothing. But

we're worried about your safety, and we don't want any more rioting."

"Then I'll stay. I like it here."

"But —"

Hobbs held up a translucent and manicured hand to command silence, polite and firm, as if he had once been somebody important. "But I'm the Antichrist, Councillor Blake. They can't harm me."

Oh boy, thought Jeff. *They're nuts, and so is he. Maybe he likes the attention. Maybe it stops him feeling so alone.* "Okay," he said carefully. "What if they come with the — er — local vicar and try to force you out with the power of God?"

For the first time Hobbs showed the faintest hint of annoyance and his forehead puckered slightly. "Now you're mocking me, Councillor Blake."

Play along. Jeff snatched an idea out of memories of Sunday School. "If you're the Antichrist, why come to Hursley Rise? Why not the Middle East?"

"It's the atmosphere." Hobbs got up and inspected the coffee pot before topping up both cups. "No, there's plenty of raw material here for me. Apathy, suspicion and cowardice. Would you call yourself a Christian, Councillor?"

"I suppose so."

"Then you probably think there's a little bit of God in all people. Personally, I think there's a little bit of *me* in everyone." He smiled engagingly, instantly a favourite uncle. "In political terms, I like to think of myself as the Opposition spokesman."

Jeff stared back at him for a while. He was, in every sense, the picture of harmless normality. Except for the young-old face, and the absence of all living things in the garden, and that cold, cold air. As Jeff stared, he could see his own breath forming wispy vapour in front of him and yet he didn't feel chilled. The clock now showed 11.15. Startled, Jeff bent his head automatically to drain his coffee cup, expecting to find it cold and the ideal cue to leave.

It scalded his mouth. He flinched.

"Still nice and hot," Hobbs said. "Shall I show you out?"

"Thank you." Jeff stood up and had to cast around him to find the door. "You'll think about what I said, though?"

"And you'll think about what I said." He smiled. "And don't worry too much about Graham Vance, will you?"

Jeff stopped, half-formed a question, and then thought better of it. He went to the window and rapped lightly on the pane with his knuckle. It was plain, ordinary, single-sheet glass – not toughened, not double-skinned. At that point he wanted to get out of the house more than anything he had ever wanted in his life.

The police car was waiting at a discreet distance.

"Bricks never break his bloody windows," said the constable driving the car. It was the first time he had spoken. "None of us want to go near the place."

They drove off. Jeff locked his hands together to stop the shaking, meshing his fingers until they went white. And his lips still burned.

\#

Letters to the Editor
Saturday April 28
Dear Sir,
Since Tuesday my life has been made a misery by these women parading up and down the streets with their children at all hours in a so-called peaceful protest. My car has been damaged and they have taken stones from my rock garden to throw at houses. I have lived at Hursley Rise for thirty years and I worked hard to buy my house to better myself. Shame on the council for not putting a stop to it.

    Yours faithfully,
    A respectable resident.

\#

Wednesday, May 2.

The chief executive's office overlooked the square and gave Jeff an excellent view of the protesters milling beneath them. On one side, Mrs Avery's army of angry women trailed by toddlers was assembling; on the other, a smaller group of people milled around with placards bearing legends like LISTEN TO THE SILENT MAJORITY ad LET US LIVE IN PEACE.

Mrs Avery's troops waved placards a little less considered in their exhortations. Jeff could see at least one with BURN THEM OUT and a child sporting a tee-shirt labelled SATEN IS AMONG US.

"I think our education initiative in Hursley might have failed, judging by the spelling," said Lennie McAndrew, and munched a chocolate biscuit. Both men stood at the window and waited. In the no-man's land between the factions, film crews and police drifted, both stopping to interview in their own manner.

"You'd think the police would clear them out," Jeff said.

"A right to peaceful protest," said Lennie. "It's not as if they've done anything."

Jeff spotted Mrs Avery giving an earnest interview to a TV reporter, waving her arm passionately in the direction of the town hall. A toddler she had been gripping by the hand wandered off unnoticed. The noise of the crowd, audible even with the windows closed, began growing from a hum into a tumult.

Something had clearly upset Mrs Avery. She broke off from the interview and elbowed her way through the crowd to where a group of Concerned Residents Against Rioters had gathered. She flung herself at a man in a red tracksuit and that was the last Jeff saw of her as the crowd began closing up and fighting broke out.

"I was afraid this would happen," said Lennie. Police could be seen as small dark blue patches struggling in the crowd, salmon swimming against the current. "It's a police matter now, Jeff. Nothing we can do." The chief executive pulled the blinds. "Time you thought about the election."

"Right now, I'd rather not."

"About Graham Vance."

Jeff felt his heart sink. "What about him?"

"Either you or I have the authority to refer the case to the police. I can understand why you might not want to do it before the election. Bear in mind that once we start the process going, we have to inform Social Services because of the child protection angle. And after that we have very little control of it."

"What are you saying exactly?"

"You might want to delay this a while – say until the end of the year."

Jeff considered it. Yes, that would be far enough from this election and far ahead enough of the next for the political damage to be minimized. But if Vance really was a risk to anyone, he had enough time to cover his tracks and continue whatever he might be doing.

Lennie seemed to interpret Jeff's silence as a prompt. "Or we could just sort it out internally. No fuss."

"Do nothing, you mean."

"Not exactly nothing – "

"You sound a lot like someone I was talking to yesterday," Jeff said, and he felt acid rise in his throat. "Maybe there really is a bit of Hobbs in us all."

Jeff went back to his own office and checked his messages. There were five threats of legal action from homeowners in Hursley Rise whose house sales had fallen through following the disturbances, and ten council tenants asking to be moved out of the area because they were afraid of reprisals.

It bothered Jeff that they called him rather than the housing department. That meant they identified him as the cause and solution to their crisis, and that boded ill for the polls on Thursday. The city was going to the dogs. And he was sure he could do nothing to stop it.

Police sirens wailed three storeys below. God only knew what the headlines would look like in the papers. Perhaps he could pull off something by lunchtime, something at the twelfth hour that would give him the front page in the evening paper. He decided to visit Mr Hobbs one last time.

#

The Antichrist was sitting by the small fishpond in his back garden. There were neither fish in it nor plants: the surface was a frozen mirror. And there were no flowers or bushes in bloom, nor any starlings or blackbirds calling.

"I can't believe I'm having this conversation," Jeff said. The coffee was black, and still did not seem to be cooling however long he left it. "But I'll ask again. Please, move out. Leave us alone and let these people try and heal their community."

Hobbs the Possible Antichrist nodded politely, a listening nod rather than an agreeing nod. "You believe them now, don't you?"

"Let's just say I've seen what you can do and the effect is the same whether you're who you say you are or not. This neighbourhood is destroyed. The buildings. Relationships. Trust. You've done it."

"I haven't done anything, Councillor Blake." Hobbs topped up his cup from the cheaply plated pot designed to look like chased silver. "I didn't have to. They did it all by themselves, and they started doing it the minute they didn't care where their kids were at night, or when they turned a blind eye to stolen goods, or even when they dumped their engine oil down the drain. That's why I didn't seek out war and unrest, Councillor. I can do my business best where people will do nothing, however small, to make things better."

"You create strife."

"It was always here."

"You've made damn sure they'll have something to fight

over."

"As I said, councillor, I've done nothing. " He smiled, a really genuine smile. "Like you. You do *nothing* quite often, don't you? There's just the one of me. It took many more humans to bring this estate to its knees, and I couldn't have done it without them."

I am having a debate with the Antichrist. Jeff grasped at a fleeting feeling of amazement. All the party coups he had survived, all the secrets and favours he held against a political rainy day, were instantly dwarfed. He had no media audience and yet he felt his sins were broadcast to the whole world.

The Antichrist's smile widened, as if he had shared Jeff's moment of revelation. "Graham Vance," he said. "Your own personal share of inaction, among many. Good day, Councillor Blake."

When he walked back down Hobbs' path again, he noticed the dead patches of grass either side of Hobbs' fence had spread to swallow up both adjoining gardens.

#

It was still a pleasant spring day, even if he did have to dodge a petrol bomb lobbed by a couple of kids. Jeff left Hursley Rise dwindling in his rear view mirror. The further he drove from the riot zone, the more normal the world became. He counted the lilac trees: one, a gap, then twos and threes, and then a wall of blossom, and the scent that drifted in through the air vents was almost sickeningly sweet. He wondered how long it would be before they dried and shrivelled, too.

He pulled into a garage to fill up. As he waited at the cash desk for his receipt, he glanced at the lunchtime edition of the local paper on the counter. ELECTIONS TOMORROW: WHO CAN SAVE THIS CITY? said the headline. "Not me," Jeff muttered, and the cashier glanced at him.

He pocketed his change and thought of Graham Vance. *You do nothing.* The taunt stung him. Nothing. And maybe he wasn't the man to save the city, either, but he had a growing feeling that there was one thing he could do, a small and selfless act that might start the world moving in another direction.

He took out his phone, thumbed through the directory and began dialling the Chief Internal Auditor. The news about Vance would probably break just as the polls opened in the morning, making up the minds of all the abstainers and don't-knows.

It had felt good being in office. He'd miss it.

DOES HE TAKE BLOOD?

(First published in *Realms of Fantasy*, August 2003. Honourable mention, Year's Best Science Fiction #21)

The lounge was too warm and too bright. It smelled of human pee, disinfectant and beeswax polish, and the plush-covered armchairs set round the edges of the room all had white crackling coverings on the seats. Ba'al Teekan Makak could hear each rustle of the plastic as the elderly occupants shifted position.

He couldn't hear so well these days, but his ears were still sharper than a human's.

"There's nothing for your father to worry about," said the social worker, talking past the demon's leathery black shoulder and folded wings as she wheeled his chair across the lounge. He gripped the armrests with his claws, fearful of being tipped out. "I know we had a little problem adjusting to the needs of the ... the *differently sentient*, but we've done lots of work with client focus groups and we're confident we can provide care that's much more *sensitive* to your father's cultural needs. We've even got a scratching post for his claws."

His offspring were behind him, following the chair as it

ploughed the thick sage green carpet. He could see them with his wrap-around vision, his night-hunter's eyes. Both youngsters looked uncomfortable.

"We can visit our sire any time?" asked his daughter.

"Course you can, dear," said the social worker. "But if you come at night, give us a call first, won't you? It might disturb the other residents." She paused, all care and cultural sensitivity, overwhelming his nostrils with a floral scent. "Now, about his special diet. Does he take blood?"

#

There were others here, not human and not exactly like him, but from the other world all the same. He could smell them. But it didn't matter anymore. When the worlds met, his kind had become subject to many human rules, as humans had changed to co-exist with his. He was in a wheelchair. He was old, an old demon who was too weak to hunt any more and now that his world had meshed with the human realm of rules and decency, he wasn't even allowed to die the quick death his offspring would have granted him in his frailty.

Gummy pale gazes watched him being wheeled into position by the bay windows. He glared back, not because he resented the rest of the home's residents, but because it was all he could do with blood-red pits for eyes.

"This is Mr Baal," said the social worker. "He's going to be staying with us now. We do music and movement on Tuesdays, Mr Baal. Would you like to join in?"

There was a time, in his youth, when he could have charred the woman's neat red curls with a single sulphurous breath. But this was no longer the time. He looked into her bright sincere face, with plump cheeks he could have chewed right off.

"That would be nice," he surrendered.

"What's your name?" said the woman to his left. She had a crocheted powder-blue bed-jacket, brown tartan slippers, a scalp you could see through her wispy white hair. Not worth eating, even if his teeth had been up to scratch.

"Ba'al Teekan Makak," he said.

"Wassat mean?"

"Lord of the Cockroaches," he said. He could see incomprehension in her nondescript, watery blue, pale-ringed eyes. "Flies was already taken."

Bed-Jacket said nothing and bent her head again. A dignified grey-bearded man in a saffron turban leaned across conspiratorially.

"They never get it right. They call me Mr Singh. They don't realise *singh* is a title, not a name. Like Baal. I'm really Anjit Singh."

"Ba'al will do fine," said the demon.

"Suit yourself," said Anjit Singh.

The afternoon was long and Teekan Makak, Lord of the Cockroaches, stared out of the bay window onto the lawn with its edging of apricot pansies. There were trees that he could have swooped through, had his back not been playing him up so much these days. Where had the last few centuries gone?

Supper was early. The staff liked to get the clearing up out of the way so they could watch TV in the lounge, said Anjit Singh. Teekan sat expectantly at the table, claws clasped in his lap, waiting for a full plate to appear on the tablemat in front of him. The mat was a laminated painting of two enchanting tabby kittens, no doubt designed to stimulate a healthy appetite.

He waited for some time. Those around him were served with pork chops, cabbage – ah, the *other* awful smell! – and mashed potato, and began tackling their meals with misshapen cutlery designed specially for gnarled arthritic hands. Just as he was beginning to think the staff had forgotten him, a care worker in a rustling gingham overall leaned close to his ear.

"Would you like to eat in your room, Mr Baal?"

"Can't I stay here?" He was fascinated by the slow-motion chewing of his fellow inmates and the precise dissection of their pork. He wanted to watch.

"I think it might upset the other residents, Mr Baal. Come on. Just until they get accustomed to you."

He nodded reluctantly and let her wheel him out to the hall where a stair lift waited at the foot of the stairs. As he passed, he saw another demon, a small forlorn grey thing, tucking in half-heartedly to a pile of mash. It met his eye and parted its lips to reveal a toothless mouth, and shrugged. How the fearsome were reduced in station, Teekan thought, and sat obediently in the lift's seat as it rattled up the stairs to the first floor.

There was a little table in his bedroom, and a washbasin and toilet in the alcove. He had a nice view over the sports centre at the back of the home. He perched on the table and ate his bowl of fresh blood and day-old chicks, watching an evening cricket match on the sports field.

It was already boring to have nothing to do and no feckless to consume, but he would see how things went. He hadn't planned on retiring at all, just a final stretch of his wings and a quick, clean end dealt by his nearest and dearest, as was proper. *We have to follow human ways now and let you retire gracefully*, his offspring had told him, as if they thought it would hinder their passage into polite society if they ripped his throat out in a civilised manner. *Social climbers*, he thought angrily, and licked the last blood out of the bowl.

He was now bored. Very bored.

He could have called a carer and asked her to take him back down to the lounge to watch the TV, just to see what humans found so magnetic about it, but he couldn't face their curiosity or their indifference. He slid under the bed, because humans never, ever wanted to look for him under there, and rocked himself to sleep.

#

Humans certainly tried to make Teekan welcome during that first month at Cherry Trees. How did he like the food? Was his room warm enough? Did he have enough to read, enough to occupy him? They never stopped consulting and monitoring quality and pressing their concern on him. And it wasn't as if he was a special case, because they cared in identical measure for all the old humans and demons in the home. He saw it.

"I was a research chemist," said Anjit.

Teekan turned a wooden puzzle in his claws, debating when to simply give up and chew it apart. "I claimed the feckless and the unwise," he said.

They both turned to stare out of the window again. "You must have been busy, then."

"It's not as if there's no call for it these days, but it's a young demon's job. Very physical."

"I had a department of fifty of the finest scientists of their generation. Now a slip of a girl changes my underwear for me."

"It's a bugger, growing old."

"It's a bugger indeed."

The world of humanity began to blossom for Teekan. True, the old ladies and even some of the old men objected to eating with him, but if he took his blood and chicks in his room and joined them later for decaffeinated coffee in front of the TV, things settled down.

Anjit taught him to play chess, because a demon could do with some patience, he said. Teekan was not one for patience and had given up on the puzzle ball, gnawing it into its component pieces.

"I can still chew some things," Teekan said, and Anjit laughed. "I am not spent yet."

At art and craft class, the care workers put Teekan with the toothless grey demon, Esaniel, and gave them clay to sculpt. They said it was good for them to be creative and keep their digits supple. Esaniel looked suspiciously at Teekan, and Teekan at him; why had the humans done this? Didn't they know the culler of the feckless and this demon – a guardian of wild places – had nothing in common? Esaniel broke the awkward silence first.

"Miss," he called, and his voice was a sigh, a gentle hiss. "Miss, can I sit with Mrs Jenkins?"

The care worker scurried up to him and bent over with her hands braced on her knees to bring her face to his. He was a very small demon. "I thought you two might like to get to know each other, having so much in common," she smiled. "Don't you like Mr Baal?"

"I don't dislike him, but. . ."

"What have we got in common?" Teekan asked, bewildered. Couldn't she see? Didn't she know?

"You're both from the demonic community," said Miss carefully.

"But we're different."

"Of course you are, dear," she said, and helped Esaniel across to Mrs Jenkins craft table, holding his hand as if he were a peculiar small boy. Teekan, puzzled, patted his clay into a mound and carved it into the form of a beetle with his fore-claw. Anjit Singh slid into the empty seat opposite him, but not before taking his handkerchief from his pocket and wiping the plastic cover.

"We're all the same to them," Anjit said. "They never think they'll end up like us."

"Well, she'll never end up like *me*," Teekan said.

"Once you're old, that's all you are – old."

"Anyone can see a demon of the wild places has different needs and wishes to the Lord of the Cockroaches. I'm urban. I like houses."

"We like the happy laughter of children, old songs round a piano, and talking about the war. Don't we?"

"No."

"No, definitely not."

"Then let us assert our individuality."

#

It was good to have Anjit around. The offspring visited less and less frequently, until by the end of August they frequently skipped a week. Well, they had a life to live, and although it saddened Teekan, it was the way of the monstrous now just as it was the way of humans. Anjit ate with him, not minding the nature of Teekan's meals, and sat in the seat next him when Cherry Trees Nursing Home took the residents on coach trips to places of interest.

And they asserted their independence together.

He and Teekan asserted their right not to take part in the old-time and ballroom dancing evenings laid on by well-meaning volunteers, because they had never liked dancing in their youth either.

"It's their way of dealing with the inevitable," Anjit said. "They're want to know someone will do the same for them one day."

"What, bore them senseless?" Teekan gazed out the window at the cherry trees, blossom long gone, fruit fallen, but leaves still intact. He wanted to prowl outside windows and crash through branches frightening the feckless and unwise, just once more. He turned to face Anjit, fixing him with his fiery stare, which had once burned much more brightly.

"I'm going to go out tonight," he said.

"They lock the doors at ten to stop us wandering around like Mrs Bishop. They had to call the police to find her."

"Go on. I just want to feel the air under my wings again." He tried to spread them, but the black leathery skin was dry and fragile and his joints cracked with the effort. "It'll upset the matron. I could have eaten her whole, once, you know."

"Okay," Anjit said. "They can't throw us out for it, can they?"

The residents were in bed by ten-thirty, seen safe in their rooms by care assistants and ticked off on a list to say they were all right. It was the sort of routine you had to have when people were of an age when they were prone never to wake up again. Teekan stuck his head out from under his bed to show the assistant he was really there.

"You sure you wouldn't be more comfortable *on* the bed, Mr Baal?" she said.

"I'm sure," he said. "Goodnight."

He waited for the footsteps to fade down the corridor and slid out onto the mat. It took a while to get up on his feet; by the time he had straightened out his limbs and wings, Anjit had eased the door open and tiptoed over to the window. It took both of them to get the sash open.

"Are you sure you can still do this?" Anjit whispered.

"Of course I can." Teekan made enough of a gap so that he could crouch on the windowsill and lean far enough forward to free his wings. He flexed them. They felt better now. He could smell the scented warmth of a late summer evening, air laden with the fragrance of mown grass and earth and living things.

He launched himself. The down-stroke of his wings lifted him off the sill and across the yard where they stored the waste bins and empty bottles, over the pine fencing and high above the sports ground. He could see the string of peach-coloured sodium lights along the motorway; he rose higher still, over the roof of the sprawling house that had been so tastefully converted into a dignified final home for older people.

Damn it, he was Ba'al Teekan Makak, scourge of the feckless. He swooped towards Mrs Jenkins' window, conveniently marked by the top growth of a climbing rose. His wing-tips scraped the window-panes and he circled to sit in the top of one of the cherry trees and watch.

After a few moments the light snapped on in Mrs Jenkins' room, creating a dusty pink square in the blackness above the twin columns of the entrance. In the still night air the commotion was audible. He waited, out of breath but exhilarated, and gulped in great lungfuls of fresh, living, *exciting* air. He remembered the wild joy of flight and how easy it had once been. Oh, it was a great life, being a demon.

He stretched his wings and let out a long howl of triumph. The window opened and Mrs Jenkins peered out. She stared at him, clearly disappointed.

"You bloody fool," she shouted. "I thought it was a cat." She slammed the window shut again and Teekan was left wondering how a cry that had once made humans foul themselves could be dismissed as caterwauling.

He thought about the unaccustomed churning in his belly, not a happy, hungry, hunting feeling but a bad emptiness. Lifting his wings, he prepared for another circuit of the home. But the wind didn't lift him, and he suddenly found himself falling, tangled in the branches, tearing his wing membranes. It hurt more than he ever remembered. He hung there for a few seconds, struggling, and the bad feeling in his stomach grew.

"Mr Baal, you get down here right away!" It was the night-duty supervisor, standing in the doorway below, framed by the bright light from the hall. "Now!"

It was easier said than done. He knew what that churning in his stomach was, now – not hunger, but humiliation.

Abandoning dignity, he fell.

#

"Mr Singh, you're his friend. You can make him see sense." Teekan listened to the conversation going on above him but not addressed to him. The matron clearly blamed Anjit for encouraging his night flights. "His flying days are over. If we don't keep him from hurting himself, we could get sued. You know we've had to report this to the Health and Safety Executive, don't you? Mr Baal's caused a *lot* of trouble."

"I know I have," Teekan cut in. "I am not deaf, although I don't hear as well as I once did, when I could hear your heartbeat from the next town and hunt you down by it. I am not stupid, although I did a stupid thing. Go care for someone else who wants it."

The matron huffed and stormed off. Anjit tucked the blanket round Teekan's legs and put his bowl of water where he could reach it from his chair.

"You can get pneumonia and die when you break bones at our age," Anjit said.

"You can sit in a chair and think you're dead already, too," Teekan said.

They lapsed into silence. Teekan had become depressed. For a while, he had thought he could adjust to a slow decline, as humans did, but he relived over and over again that moment when he went from soaring flight to a tangled heap on the ground, helpless like quarry. It was no way for a demon to meet the Other One.

"I think I'd like to sit in my room," he said. "Alone."

One of the assistants wheeled him into the service lift, settled him in his room and gave him a couple of ibuprofen tablets. She positioned him by the window. He gazed out listlessly and noticed a row of garlic cloves placed carefully along the sill, end to end.

"What's that there for?" he asked.

The assistant fussed with the blanket and put a magazine on his lap. "To stop you going for a spin, of course. You can't cross over garlic, can you?"

Teekan stared up at her in bewilderment, and then hissed in disgust, the hiss of a steam locomotive.

"That's *vampires*, you foolish girl. I'm not a vampire. I'm Ba'al Teekan Makak. We are *not* all the same, do you hear me?" He reached out for a chunk of garlic and crunched it defiantly in front of her. "And no silver bullets or holy water, either. No, I do *not* take blood, which I could have told you had you asked me."

He waited for her to scuttle from the room and shut the door before he howled and howled and then wept sulphur tears that spluttered and hissed on his cheeks.

#

The leaves on the cherry trees had browned and fluttered to the ground, and a young lad in a denim jacket raked them into neat piles. Teekan watched for a while. He was not hungry, and he was not interested. He wanted to fly again.

Just once more. That was all.

"I will not help you do this," Anjit said. He sounded more frightened and upset than angry. Teekan knew the frightened sounds humans made, because he had heard them often. His friend gripped his arm. As always, human hands felt cold, as if they were already dead.

"Then don't stop me," Teekan said.

"You can live many more years here. I'll be here, Esaniel will be here. We can have a little fun. A few laughs."

He meant well. He was a very good friend, for a human. Teekan returned the squeeze on his arm. "I can *exist* here. But to live, I have to fly, and I can't fly any more."

"And I can't do handstands any more, but I don't want to die because of it."

"Well, that's you. And I'm me. And demons who can no longer hunt go gladly to the Other One. I collected more feckless and unwise than any before me, and I would now like to collect my reward in the Great Below."

Anjit's eyes welled with tears. He patted Teekan's arm and stood up. "I am truly sorry. Perhaps you will feel better in a while. Would you rather be alone now?"

Teekan nodded. He wanted to tell Anjit that he had made a dismal time more bearable, and that there were some things that the kingdom of the monstrous did a lot better than the realm of humans, such as knowing when a cycle was completed. But he thought Anjit might be more upset if he did.

Teekan never thought he would find himself sparing a human's feelings.

#

The sun had just a few minutes to sink to the horizon. It was a fine evening with an amber sunset and Teekan watched the shadows lengthen from his window. It had taken him ten minutes to force the sash up enough to get through it.

There was a knock on the door, then the door-knob rattled. "Teekan?" Anjit called. "Teekan, why have you locked the bloody door? Open up!"

The breeze was cool on his face. He tested his wings, squatting on the sill. It was amazing what ibuprofen could do even for a demon. His joints felt supple. The fact that it was temporary didn't matter now.

"I'm going for a *flight*," he shouted. "Just look at that sky!"

And Teekan jumped.

He rose over the yard and the pine fence, a demon again. He had only a few hundred yards left in him, but it was enough, and it was a lovely, lovely evening. He climbed higher, as high as he could go until his lungs strained to cope, and then and banked towards the sports ground, down towards the velvet-perfect cricket pitch. His speed was increasing to terminal velocity. It would be quick.

He was not just any old demon. He was Ba'al Teekan Makak. And he wondered what rewards the Great Below had in store for him.

THE LAST PENNY

(First published in *Spaceways Weekly*, 2000. Readers' Choice award for August 2000. The worst thing about writing dystopian fiction is that you think you're going further than any government would, and then you realise you haven't even scratched the surface of reality...)

They said co-ordination was one of the first things to go with age, but she could still lob a coin into a crumpled coat from a fair distance. She could, of course, have walked closer to the down-and-out, but his dog – a surprisingly well-fed thing given its station in life – looked capable of lunging in a split second.

"Thanks love," said the recipient of her charity. A young man: obligatory stringy hair and a grimy once-yellow sweater. "Don't you want a copy of the magazine, then?"

She paused, a reflex at being addressed. So he wasn't begging. He was selling. He held up a copy from his cross-legged position, and she could easily pick out *Still The Big Issue* on the masthead.

"No thanks," she said. "But you will get yourself something to eat, won't you?"

The young man, the sort that made her feel uncomfortable, gave her a half-hearted salute and ruffled his dog's coat.

Christine always had coins and banknotes on her. She

liked old money. In a month's time, real currency would cease to be legal tender: there would be no more ecus and pounds and eurodollars, neither in coinage nor note. There would be nothing to drop in a charity tin, or leave under the plate in a restaurant, or save in a jar. Nothing to wish with, or toss to win. Everything, absolutely everything would finally be charged to the barc, the barcode embedded for eternity into the heel of your hand. The public information jingles were now interrupting pretty well everything she watched on TV, urging her to make sure she'd banked all her currency by the end of the year.

She stood in the queue at the seitan bar with her daughter – the married one – waiting for a table. Infobites flashed across the screen at head height, suggesting where they might want to shop next, and there was the obligatory countdown to the withdrawal of currency. "Thirty days to spend it!" a voice trilled. Christine made an irritated sucking noise between her teeth.

"I don't understand why you're so awkward about using the damn thing," said her daughter. "We've had charge cards for nearly a century. You do your grocery shopping on line. What's so wrong with a damn barc?"

"Choice," said Christine. "There's enough data stored on me to fill a library. I want to be able to buy a bar of chocolate without anyone knowing about it, except me and the chocolate."

"Yes, and I want to know that you're not in danger of being mugged for cash and cards when you go out, and that if you have an accident the paramedics will know who you are and what medication you're on. I think that's a small price to pay for some marketing firm finding out that you eat Ritter marzipan bars."

Christine raised her hand slowly. It looked for all the world like a slow-motion martial arts movement, preparing for a downward chop: faint grey lines and dots showed through the translucent skin from the base of her little finger to the wrist.

"There, I'm branded," she said. "My whole life encoded. Maybe they'll chop my hand off when they rob me."

"Please use it, Mum. I hate you carrying all that money around."

"Well, they'd better mug me in the next thirty days, or they're wasting their time," said the older woman defiantly. She changed the subject. "How much longer are they going to keep us waiting for a table?"

For all the ritual warfare with her daughter Dennie, Christine liked shopping. Ordering at home was nice, but recreational shopping satisfied the primal gatherer still lurking in her. Talking to real live shop assistants was fun: they didn't have advice to give and even if they thought she was a doddering old woman they kept it to themselves. Waiters were good company, too. The boy who served her mock duck and realistically-shaped seitan ribs gave her extra dipping sauce with a big grin.

Christine left him a crisp twenty-ecu bill by way of a tip. Dennie tutted.

"Between me and him, dear," Christine smiled. "Between me, and him, and nobody else."

#

"What did you get?" asked her daughter. The grandchildren were safely elsewhere, and the two of them could discuss Christmas presents without fear of discovery.

"A hand-bag," Christine said. She held up a ludicrously tiny satin drawstring bag, scarcely big enough for a lipstick and comb. "Jill's that age now, isn't she?" She fished a few coins from the large pickle jar on the mantelpiece and put them in the bag.

"Mum?"

"It's bad luck to give a bag or a purse without a coin in it," she said. "Indulge me, Dennie."

"I hope you're going to put all that in your account before the deadline."

"I've got a while yet."

"Even so, don't forget, will you?"

"It's been such a habit," said Christine. "Ever since I was Jill's age. I always saved coins. It made me feel safe, like there was always something there in an emergency."

"Well, at least nobody's likely to break in and steal them now." Dennie spoke in the tone of someone who had forgotten her mother had once held a management post, and was quite certain that old age happened only to other people, and unlucky or foolish ones at that.

"Help me empty them out," Christine said. "I'm going to count them."

The two women heaved the jar off the shelf and almost dropped it before rolling it over on the hand-carved rug. The coins spilled out in a sharp-smelling avalanche. There was a mix of silver and bimetal and bronze, and they took a lapful each and began counting, awkwardly, piling up little towers of the same denomination. They were so silently engrossed for so long that Jill put her head round the door to see what they were doing and was shooed away.

"Two hundred and thirty six ecus and some small change," Dennie said. "Let's bag it up and I'll pay it in to the bank for you."

"No," Christine said. "It's not a fortune. I'll have some fun with it. Just bag it up in tens for me, would you, please?"

"You're getting very careless with your money – "

"I'm not senile. I just want to have some fun."

"Alright, have it your way," said her daughter.

#

The stringy yellow lad and his dog were still in their position by the perfumery when she went shopping a few days later. Christine waved to him and made a mental note to empty the contents of her coin jar: he would at least have a few weeks to spend it in.

She walked on to the delicatessen and browsed through

the cheeses. It was a protest. Not an energetic or hazardous one, the sort she itched to try in her fit and able youth, but a protest nonetheless. She asked for a slab of unpasteurised Brie, silently blessed the anarchic French for defying conventional food hygiene, and paid for it with her barc.

"I really did think the wrinkles would stop the machine reading my hand," she said, and laughed, and the assistant forced a smile. "Used to happen all the time when I was a kid. Machines couldn't read wrinkled bar-codes."

But it wasn't a simple laser job, the barc. Her entire life was in those tiny chips. The medical information talked to the pharmacy and the pharmacy talked to the bank and the bank talked to her insurers and her insurers talked to next of kin, all in the microscopic confines of the heel of her hand. She found a bench nearby, sat down and flipped open her personal messager to see who might have called.

"CHRISTINE EBLEY," it scolded in capitals on the screen. "YOU'VE MADE A FOOD PURCHASE. THE CALCIUM CONTENT WILL HELP YOU AVOID OSTEOPOROSIS THE NATURAL WAY. BUT THE FAT CONTENT AND THE LACK OF PASTEURISATION IS NOT RECOMMENDED FOR A PERSON WITH YOUR HEALTH PROFILE. IF YOU WOULD LIKE ADVICE ON A HEALTHIER ALTERNATIVE, PLEASE PRESS HERE. FROM YOUR HEALTH MONITORING SERVICE."

Christine raised the messager to her lips and smiled. "Reply," she said. "Dear Monitor. I know it's bad for me but mind your own business and let me die happy. Send."

It wouldn't even be read by a human being, but it made her feel better. She'd made a stand. Sometimes, even at 75, she wanted people to know they couldn't take her compliance for granted.

"Good on you, missus," said a voice, and she looked up and into the face of Yellow Stringy, passing by with his dog trotting sedately behind.

"They do get to me, sometimes," she said. "Silly of me –

anyway, would you like this?" She held out the pack of cheese. "I imagine you don't get enough calcium either."

Yellow Stringy smiled, a genuinely embarrassed and little-boy smile, and took the cheese with a polite nod. "Well, I don't eat it, but Herbert does."

Herbert reacted to the enunciation of his name with a dignified sideways tilt of his square head. He looked like he had a substantial dose of bull terrier in him. Christine broke off an oozing piece of the Brie and held it out to the dog, who took it with the delicacy of a poodle.

"He's what my mother would have called a lord mayor's fool," she said. "He's a bit of a gourmet, your Herbert."

"He's getting on a bit now."

"And you get his left-overs, right?"

"He's my best mate. I look after him first."

Stringy's heart was in the right place, she decided. Herbert took the remainder of the Brie piece by piece.

"They've always got some file on you, haven't they?" Stringy said, indicating the barc on her hand.

"Oh, my daughter worries. She thinks I'm totally senile." She leaned a little closer to him, confidentially, and was surprised that he didn't smell bad. "She signed me up to this medical monitor service because of my heart. I don't mind having my cardiac implant monitored 24 hours, and I can just about cope with them being able to tell exactly where I am, but I draw the line at them checking my damn groceries every time."

"I haven't got one."

"Cardiac implant? I'd hope not."

"No, a barc. I'm strictly cash. I don't want to be spied on every move I make."

"And you don't have a regular salary to charge anything to, I suppose."

"Nah. I'm outside this society. And that's fine by me."

"What if you need it one day?"

"I've opted out. I'll take what comes with that."

"And when currency is phased out?"

Stringy paused for a few seconds. "Barter," he said.

"You've still got a few weeks," Christine said, and pressed a bag of change into his hand.

"I'm not begging," he said.

"I know. I'm shedding assets. Take it."

Stringy cupped his hand round the bag and looked as if he might actually start crying. Christine felt uneasy.

"Go on," she said. "Go and get a good meal. Or open a bank account."

"I think I'll go for the meal," he said. He got up and Herbert sprang up from his sprawl to follow him. He turned.

"Thank you," he said. "You're a very kind lady."

#

At the monorail stop, Christine wondered about Stringy's future a little longer and then heard the incoming whirr and rush of air of the approaching carriages. The doors opened. "Fareham Central," she said, and brushed the bar-coded heel of her hand across the sensor pad so her fare could be charged automatically to her account. "Thank you, Christine Ebley," said a disembodied voice. She didn't care for that: she thought she was entitled to anonymity on a rail journey. But it was the way things were, and nobody cared who she was anyway, so she sat at the front, where a driver would have been in her youth and savoured the sheer-drop view of the harbour beneath her.

At least she no longer had to fumble for the exact change. Modern banking had its advantages.

#

Twenty bags of change were heavy. Christine took two or three with her when she went out, and the pressure on her shoulder was enough to encourage her to spend as fast as she could. It was what her mother had called "silly money", money you wouldn't miss if it were all gone with nothing to show for it, a smallish sum to be frittered for the hell of it if you were accustomed most days to watching every penny. There was real pleasure in a small burst of irresponsibility. Like buying the cheese, listeria-ridden or not, it was an act of assertion. *I am alive, still. I can still choose.*

She took a handful of coins and fed them into the maw of the charity box. She took another handful and dropped them in the ornamental fountain that stood at the crossroads of the mall, and wished.

For what? She'd had her wishes. She closed her eyes briefly and wished that the grandchildren grew up strong and healthy, and that all the people like Stringy could feel part of her society.

And she still had more than a dozen bags of change left.

The next day, she loaded them into a shopping trolley. She hadn't used one for years, and resisted them fiercely, believing they were the ultimate admission that she was truly past it. But the coins were heavy. She rumbled the trolley behind her, faintly satisfied at getting her own back on young roller-bladers and dawdlers, and found Stringy and Herbert seated like Buddhas outside the perfumery.

"John," she said. She knew that much about him now, but she still thought of him as Stringy. "Want to help an old woman blow her last penny?"

"You're a one, you know that?" he said, and the three of them wandered off for tea and cakes, a pot of Nilgiri and slabs of Sachertorte and macadamia slices: nothing less would do. It was something, somewhere, that neither of them should have done or been, and it was all the more enjoyable for that.

"Before you spend it all, there's something you might like to see," Stringy said.

"Yes?" She wrapped remnants of cake in a napkin to carry out to Herbert, who was waiting with elderly canine dignity outside the tea shop.

"The bloke with the antiques shop's got loads of old slot machines," he said. "And vending machines. He's doing it to sort of celebrate the end of currency. He's even got ones that take pennies."

"Oh, God, I remember those!" Christine was enthralled. It rekindled memories of thumping chocolate bar machines that wouldn't yield their bounty, and of waxed paper cartons of flavoured milk that plummeted from the machine on the old town railway station. They always fell with a huge thud, and the milk so ice-cold it hurt when she gulped it down. "Let's go," she said.

#

They fed the hungry machines and laughed like kids. There were games older than she was, where you rolled coins on a board and tried to land them on a winning square. There were old fruit machines, which had been adapted to take several changes of coinage over their lives. There were machines that offered prizes if you could operate a miniature mechanical grabber. And they played them all, until they were tired, and left laughing to find somewhere for another cup of tea.

Christine wondered if she had overdone it. She was tired: a bench nearby was inviting her to be sensible and accept she was old for a while. They sat down, and she rubbed Herbert's head while he rested it against her leg.

"I do worry about you, John," she said.

"Why?"

"What's going to happen to you when you can't spend cash any more?"

He shrugged. "Like I said. I decided I didn't want to be tracked and analysed every time I bought something or went somewhere. I'll put up with whatever I have to, long as I don't have to have a barc. And that means I can't work, because I can't be paid by credit transfer, so I'll have to think of something."

"It might be okay while you're young and fit," Christine said. "But what are you going to do when you get old? When you need the sort of things the barc can hook you up to?"

"I'll worry about that when it happens," he said.

"Okay. Then have this."

It was the last seven bags of change, most of it large denominations. He looked at it and then at her.

"John, do something sensible with it, will you?" she said.

He smiled. "I'll try."

She was going to get up but she felt the need to sit a little longer. Indigestion was gnawing at her chest.

"I don't think I should have eaten that nut slice," Christine said. "Nuts. Always hard to digest…"

It really was just an indigestion pain. It had to be. She felt hot and sticky: then there was nausea and the pain crept up the left side of her neck, to her jaw. She began to admit to herself it wasn't the nuts giving her so much trouble, and evidently so did Stringy, because he had started talking very fast and trying to make her stay still.

"Breathe," he kept saying. "Just breathe. God, I think we'd better get you some help."

People stopped and came closer. She was aware of them at the edge of her vision. They didn't come close enough to help, just to stare. "Christ, I've got to call someone," Stringy was saying. "Where are the bloody coin phones? Jesus, where are they?" And the pain got worse, and she could only see the pattern of her skirt on her lap, and hear some older man telling Stringy to sod off and leave the old lady alone.

But he's trying to help me, she wanted to say. The pain stopped her. *He's trying to call for an ambulance. He can't because he can't pay for a call because he hasn't got a barc and I knew, damn well knew, that barc might be the death of me in the end —*

She had no idea how long she had sat crumpled there. But she did know Stringy hadn't sodded off at all, and was still there. He kept apologising. He kept saying sorry all the time, right up to the point where she felt professional hands unfold her and someone ask if she could hear them.

"No, and you can't take the dog in the ambulance either," someone said. The mask was on her face, something popped briefly against the back of her hand a few times and she was lifted, lifted into somewhere brightly lit and boomingly hollow.

The pain was easing. She stared up at the bewildering roof of the ambulance and knew that she would never hear the end of it from Dennie. The medical monitor service had done its job. No call had been necessary: its vigilance was unceasing, deep in her chest, and it had alerted the hospital. She was tagged, timed and marked: the paramedics knew exactly what was wrong, where she was and the first-stage treatment she needed even before they set off.

The bloody thing had saved her life.

#

"Where's Herbert?" Christine asked.

Stringy stood at her bedside with a neat bunch of bronze chrysanthemums. She got the feeling it was the only bunch of flowers he'd bought in his adult life. His hair was scraped back into a ponytail, and he was wearing a shirt and trousers under a shiny new track jacket.

"Had to leave him with security," Stringy said. "No dogs, except in the hospice wing."

"And I'm not heading there yet."

"No." He looked around the room as if seeking permission from invisible nurses before pulling up a chair and sitting down. "So how are you?"

"Fine. A minor heart attack. Not my first. They've had a bit of a poke around through an artery and replaced some dead tissue. I'll be out in a day or so."

"God, Mrs E, you could have died."

"*Could* have."

"And a lot of use I was. I couldn't even find a phone I could use."

"You didn't need to." She tapped her chest. "I can't make a move without my minder tracking me."

Stringy laid the chrysanthemums on the bedside table. He

was certainly very neat. It robbed him of the air of menace he'd seemed to have when she first saw him. He was just a lad. Bewildered, down on his luck, defiant towards just about everything – except her.

"I see you spent your money sensibly," she said, indicating the clothes. She glanced down and checked: even shiny new shoes.

"I'm back among the humans now," he said.

And he held out his right hand, edgeways on, in that combat gesture that divided the safe-spending, monitored, secure majority from the unregistered. He had a brand new barc implanted into his hand.

"Well, welcome to the oppressed masses, John," she said. "What made you give in?"

"Because I was helpless when you collapsed. Because I'm afraid there'll be no sensor to catch me when I'm really sick. All sorts of things." He smiled. She realised she had no idea what his surname was. "So I got myself registered and I've got on a job training course."

They looked at each other for a long time, not saying anything or even feeling the need to. Christine knew he was feeling a little defeated, as she had done when she accepted she needed a shopping trolley, or eyesight correction. "You haven't really sacrificed your freedom," she said. "Freedom's pretty cold and lonely sometimes. Besides – now we're all chipped up, they've got too much data on their hands to bother the likes of us, haven't they?"

"Yeah." He fished in his pocket. "Anyway, here's a get well present."

He hadn't wrapped it. It was a couple of bars of her favourite chocolate. "Cash – they'll never trace it to you," he said, and laughed. He took something else out of his pocket and laid it on her lap. "A souvenir."

She held the white metal chain up and admired the polished penny coin gleaming in the light. It was pierced through near the rim, so that it didn't hang straight. She realised he had done it himself.

"Defacing coins of the realm, eh?" she said. She eased the necklace over her head. "Thank you."

"My mum used to say about good people that they would give you their last penny," Stringy said. "You gave me yours. So I'm giving you mine."

"You're a decent lad, John."

"When you're out of here, do you want to have tea in the mall sometime?"

"Oh, yes," Christine said. "I'd love to. I would like that very much."

She watched him go, a little awkward in the clothes of the regular and registered, anxious to collect Herbert from the security staff. And she toyed with the penny on the chain, and knew she wouldn't really miss hard cash at all.

ORCHIDS

(First published in *Neverworlds,* 1999. I;d seen a documentary on AIS and it struck me as the ideal topic for an identity story. It must have been one of the first short stories I wrote.)

An expensive, embossed card, cattleya orchids picked out in the palest pink. "To my special girl, with love from your Dad. Happy Birthday. We are what
 we're meant to be."

"Oh, Dad, I miss you so much."
Simon scrambled up the attic ladder. "Who are you talking to. Mum?"
"Just remembering my Dad, love," Vicky said. She put the card back in a
 manila envelope that was sueded with age and frequent handling. Her life was in those carefully-kept cards. "I like to remember sometimes."

#

"Congratulations. It's going to be a boy."
Bob looked up at the doctor and wanted to tell him that

he bloody well expected it to be for the money he'd paid. Instead, he smiled his best paternal smile and squeezed Gina's hand. It was clenched tight. He squeezed it anyway.

"It might be premature to tell everyone just yet," the doctor said.

"Implantation's been successful, and there's no reason to suppose Gina won't carry to term. But let's be cautious."

"I feel like I did the last time." Gina looked determined rather than

elated. "It's going to be okay."

"Of course it will." The doctor ushered them towards the receptionist.

"Let's make some appointments for you, shall we?"

Bob had no intention of announcing their pregnancy to the world. It was something he was hoping to avoid for as long as possible. He didn't want to lie. But he didn't want to admit to anyone, especially Gina's mother, that they had paid for IVF treatment and genetic manipulation.

"We'll have to tell her it's a boy sooner or later," Gina said. "Or we'll

slip up and call it 'he' sooner or later. Yes, when we do tell her we'll have to say she's going to have another grandson."

#

Ten weeks.

"Yes, mum. . .yes, that's right, I'm pregnant. . . no, I didn't tell you. . . no, I didn't want to get everyone's hopes up. . .it's private. . . I'm sorry, really I am, but it's okay now, you can tell everyone. . ."

Bob heard Gina put the phone down and sigh theatrically.

"Can I say interfering old cow?" he called.

"You can," she called back.

"Interfering old cow."

Gina flopped down onto the sofa and took an apple from the fruit bowl beside her. "She thinks I should have told her we were trying."

"Hello mum, just calling to let you know Bob's spent us up to the hilt getting a private clinic to give me IVF and mess with the embryo to make sure we have a boy like Jack, by way of recompense."

"You know she didn't really blame you for that. Let's not re-open – "

"If I had filled in the pond, like she said, Jack would still be here."

"She never meant that. It was grief talking."

"She meant it."

"I'm not going to encourage you. I'm not even going to start that argument again."

"Thank Christ she's at the other end of the country."

"Yes, but her mouth's on the other end of the phone, and the news'll be halfway round the world by now."

"Did you know you're thirty-six and you don't have to ask your mum's permission any more?"

"Really?" She snorted a laugh and lobbed the neatly chewed core into the waste bin. "Tell her, will you?"

Gina's family were funny about children. They didn't produce many. Maiden

aunts and female cousins who had failed in the past to procreate were still spoken of with pity at Hickson family gatherings. When he and Gina had tried for six years to conceive, it seemed they were due to be the next holders of the Hickson Award for Failing in Reproductive Duty.

The obsession had given Jack's arrival an almost religious significance. It also made his death even more tragic, if such a thing were possible.

"I'll make some tea," Bob said. As he passed the dresser in the hall, the repeating video picture caught his eye and he tried not to look at it.

It was Jack on his green tricycle, gleeful at discovering he could turn the handlebars and actually move in another direction. He'd been three. A year later, he'd drowned in the garden pond

Bob was finding it increasingly hard lately to meet Jack's unseeing gaze, reproduced over and over again by the video portrait. *We're not replacing you, I promise, Jack-Jack. There'll never be anyone to replace you. We just wanted another boy like you.* He turned the frame slightly so Jack's gaze wasn't directly aimed at him, but stopped short of turning it completely to the wall. Gina wouldn't like that.

"What're you doing?" she called. "I thought you were supposed to be waiting on me now I'm pregnant."

"Sorry, love. Tea coming up."

#

Twelve weeks.

A pale blue check teddy playing with a duckling on idealised grass, a blue ribbon threaded through the card. Cursive script saying "It's a boy!" with the words "going to be" inserted in cousin Fiona's handwriting. "Congrats, Bob and Gi! Have you got a name for him yet?"

"John," Bob said to the card, and put it back on the Victorian mantelpiece.

"She thinks I've had an amniocentesis to find out the gender," Gina said, and moved the card a little to the left. "I don't feel like telling her."

"Why?" Bob asked.

"She'll accuse me of trying to have designer babies. She hates this test-tube stuff."

"Petri dish."

"You're so pedantic."

"It fascinates me. It's just so crude and kid's chemistry set, isn't it? They can make a baby out of the bits and manipulate the chromosomes and build a boy. And they do it in a glass saucer. I find that – oh, I don't know. Nicely ironic."

"So – we admit we had IVF. But we don't admit we specified a male embryo, or its colouring and appearance."

"Well, it'll avoid the argument with your family about the destruction of spare embryos."

"And we'll just have a row about interfering with nature and distorting the gender balance and trying to replace Jack instead."

"Your call."

The method might have been a controversial one among the more traditional members of their families, but everyone appeared to approve of their having another child as soon as possible. It was good for them, they said. Bob tolerated the inane reassurances of with ill-concealed irritation: how could it be good for them to have another baby quickly and get over it? How could you erase a person you loved and believe that a different one – even one you would grow to adore – could fill their place? It was all part of the repertory of foolish sympathies trotted out by the ignorant, just another phrase that slotted somewhere between time being a great healer and that Jack would always be alive in their hearts.

No, Jack was gone forever. John was coming.

#

Sixteen weeks.

They decided to call him John sometime between the news that the embryo appeared healthy and normal, and that implantation had been successful. The rigorous schedule of trips to the clinic and injections and providing samples gave way to antenatal check-ups and relaxation classes. It still felt regimented to Bob.

Gina lay on the couch, craning her neck to see the grainy image on the screen beside her. The gynaecologist – "Call me Doug" – rolled the ultrasound sensor over her swelling belly with one hand, and pointed out interesting detail on screen with the other. Bob watched, bewildered. It could have shown the wreck of the Bismarck for all he knew.

"Look," said Dr Doug. "That's his spine you can see there – and he's moving around."

"Oh, Bob, look!" Gina said.

Bob looked. There was a little rapid blip-blip-blip at the centre of the image: a tiny heartbeat. That much he could understand, and suddenly the John-to-be was real for him. He had a son.

Or another son. Jack would never stop being his firstborn, his eldest. He owed him that. He scolded himself for not prefacing the thought with that qualifier, his second son. I'm not replacing you, Jack-Jack, he thought.

"We'll get a picture or two for you," Dr Doug said. "Yes – you've definitely got a boy, but you knew that, didn't you? Silly of me. Look. Those are the

testes. See that? You can definitely buy blue romper suits now, Mrs Fraser."

#

A no-particular occasion card, in lieu of a letter. A scrap of an autumn woodland scene. "Gina, Bob sounded dreadful when I phoned last night. Is he all right? I know we've had our differences but he ought to be looking forward to the birth. Perhaps I upset him talking about Jack. Call me, will you? Love, Mum."

Thirty-eight weeks.
It was a huge store. Bob didn't like the idea of Gina shopping for things so close to the birth but she was determined. "It's not an illness," she said.

"Okay, I'll believe that when you refuse an epidural," he said. He steered her between the racks of cute little pink dresses and powder-blue dungarees, feeling like a mahout driving a she-elephant. One wrong step, he thought, and her momentum would take an aisle of goods with her. "Admit you're not so fast on your feet, will you?"

"They've got a coffee shop,' Gina said. "I could do with a sit-down." She shifted uncomfortably in her seat while they picked over sandwiches and coffee. "I'll be glad to get rid of this permanent indigestion," she said, and pressed the heel of her hand against her chest. "It's all a bit crowded in here."

"Not long now."

"You don't seem very happy lately. What's wrong?"

"The usual." Bob busied himself rummaging through the bags of stuffed toys and other brightly-coloured things designed to enchant a baby. He had avoided buying a furry monkey. Jack had loved his too much. "You know. Whether we can go through this without trying to make him into Jack."

Gina had set her lips in what he thought of as her line of no surrender. It wasn't a new debate. "I'm not going to go through all that again."

"Well, how are we going to stop ourselves comparing and remembering? It's bound to happen. We're going to see him at all the stages we saw Jack at. We're going to call him Jack sooner or later. He's going to have brown hair and blue eyes and he's going to look like Jack, too. Is he ever going to move out of that shadow, Gi?"

"It'll be different when he arrives."

His father had said as much. Bob didn't share many close moments with his father: but the old man had listened without embarrassment to Bob's fears about treating Jack as a commodity to be replaced, about unconsciously moulding John into Jack's shape, about just doing things wrong. "Kids grow up the way they want and there's bugger all you can do about it in the end," he told him. It was as near as Fraser senior had ever come to philosophy.

"Uh," Gina said suddenly.

"What's up, love? Not the pains starting?"

"Oh." She stared down at her lap, jaw slack. "Oh no."

Bob stood up and the chair scraped back noisily behind him. He started fumbling for his mobile, ambulance and hospital numbers already on auto-dial. "It's okay. Don't worry —"

He heard before he saw. Drip, drip, trickle on the easy-clean tile floor.

"My waters have broken," Gina said, matter-of-fact again. "I didn't get any warning of that. Oh, shit..."

It was a busy Saturday and the traffic was gridlocked as usual. Bob knew the ambulance would be a long time arriving, but that didn't seem to bother the shop staff, who cleared a space in an office and summoned one of their colleagues.

"We get this all the time," one of them told Bob. She was gathering wipes and cloths and other things he couldn't take in right then. "Pregnant customers, rotten traffic – this is our sixth birth, I think. We can hold the fort until the medics show up, don't worry."

Gina was swearing fluently. Bob offered his hand but she batted him away. John Edward Fraser came into the world while his father listened to the wailing siren of an ambulance making slow progress in the street outside. The child joined in with a thin chorus that rose to braying crescendo.

"Oh! Lovely!" The shop assistant who could turn her hand to obstetrics folded a towel around the new-born and beamed at Bob and the sobbing Gina. "A lovely little girl!"

#

Bob stared at the screen of his mobile. He was scrolling the news headlines, phone numbers and home-shopper pages, but he couldn't see any of it. He could hear Dr Doug. He couldn't hear Gina. He found himself shaking his head involuntarily.

"Androgen insensitivity syndrome is pretty rare," said the doctor. "I think

your baby is what we call a CAIS – complete AIS. None of his male hormone receptors will function no matter how much testosterone is in his system."

"All foetuses have the characteristics of both sexes at first and then one

or the other dominates and you end up with a boy or a girl. We all have cells that switch on and do things when the right hormone touches them. In this case, the cells that are supposed to make male characteristics like genitalia and body hair just don't react to male hormones at all. So the child looks female, even though it has male chromosomes."

Bob found himself staring at Dr Doug's white clogs. A small fleck of blood marked the leather: it seemed a weird choice of footwear with green surgical overalls. "But it's more than that, isn't it?" he said. "I mean, is it just a technical thing or is – she actually ill?"

"The baby's got no uterus but is otherwise perfectly healthy. The good news is that there's a reasonable vaginal structure, so – alright, she might not need a great deal of surgery to have something of a normal life as a female." Dr Doug stared at Bob for a few seconds and then turned to Gina, as if he was expecting a comment. None came. "I realise how hard this must be for you. I think the important thing is to concentrate on the baby. It's not going to be any easier for her when she'd old enough to understand."

"We tell her what she is?" Gina said at last.

"It's probably best," Dr Doug replied. "It'll be apparent to her at puberty. No periods, probably no pubic hair. If she grows up knowing she's a little different, it'll save her a great deal of trauma. I do assume you accept she's best reassigned as a female."

Bob glanced at Gina. She was fumbling with the small card delivered to the ward with a bouquet from her sister.

"You said we had a boy," she said.

"And you did. The karyotype – sorry, the chromosomes were XY, which is male."

"And the scan."

"It's easy to mistake the labia for testes if that's what you're expecting to see. And you can test for the carrier, but you have to know that's what you're looking for, and this is a one in 20,000 chance at best, maybe much lower."

"Carrier?" Gina sounded insulted. "Me?"

"Have you any female relatives who didn't have children or didn't appear to ever have a relationship?"

"Great aunts and a cousin, some way back."

"There's a chance they had it. Remember that this wasn't

well understood and many AIS cases went undiagnosed."

Bob knew what Gina was thinking, and it wasn't medical. She had to be

worrying about what they would tell the family, how they would explain that they conceived a boy and somehow gave birth to a girl.

It was going to be a nightmare. This would almost certainly be the last

child they'd have at this time of their lives. A child who couldn't give them grandchildren: the end of the Fraser line, oddly enough, but not of the Hicksons. Bob, an only child, had most to lose on the dynastic front. He had expected to be angry and afraid and threatening legal action once the shock had worn off, but instead he found himself relieved. He hadn't replaced Jack at all. He'd had a daughter. And that was curiously comforting.

"I don't expect you'd thought of a girl's name,' Dr Doug said. They watched the nurse bring the baby back into the ward from the latest batch of tests and lay her in Gina's arms.

"Joanna Victoria," Bob said. It occurred to him much later that he hadn't even consulted Gina on the choice.

#

Nine years seven months.

"Hope you're feeling better soon." A bright yellow card with daft cartoons, which plays clips from the century's funniest comedy shows. "With love from Dad."

The best thing about being self-employed as far as Bob was concerned was not having work-mates to talk to. As a management consultant, he came and went. He never needed to explain why he needed a day off to take Vicky to hospital or what was wrong with her.

There was nothing wrong with her. She was just different.

Bob had been the one to call her Vicky. Joanna had been

an unthinking response at the time, but it was a poor name, a substitute boy's name dressed up to fit, and he preferred something uncompromisingly feminine. It struck him only later that it was another feminised male label, by which time it had stuck.

The capacity of children to tolerate medical procedures astounded him, and it was a topic he often discussed with other parents from the AIS support group. Two of them lived close enough to contact personally. Bob found he was growing more inclined to talk to them than to Gina, and Gina was more distant about it than ever since she had discovered one of them was a single mother.

"How's it going?" Janice asked.

Bob rearranged the individual teapots and delicate patisserie on the tray, fearful of a slip and the clatter of falling china. It was a genteel coffee shop. "Pretty good, I think."

They found a table overlooking the river and neither much cared if anyone they knew saw them together. It was not a place for assignations, more a shoppers' way station. "Is Vicky still on implants?"

"They don't seem to bother her, and at her age they're better than oestrogen patches," Bob said. "They don't fall off, anyway. Do you want sugar? I didn't get any."

"No sugar. How's your wife taking it?"

"So so."

"It can be tough."

"I thought she'd identify with Vicky. Mother daughter bond. But it's just getting more distant."

"Guilt. And Vicky's a pretty glamorous girl in the making, so don't confuse female rivalry with something special to AIS."

"No, it's guilt. We asked for it. We found a doctor and paid him to create a child for us and it went wrong, and Vicky's paying the price for our covetousness. We wanted a possession."

"I don't think this is a visitation from God, Bob. AIS is rare, nothing to do with IVF."

"Well, I feel guilty. We have way too many choices over fertility these days." Suddenly he didn't feel like tackling the millefeuille pastry in front of him. It looked both daunting and fragile. "She wouldn't have happened if I hadn't paid for it. I never felt right about it, you know – but I went from feeling guilty about trying to replace a lost son to feeling guilty about bringing a damaged daughter into the world."

"Is that how you see her? Damaged?"

"She's had a gonadectomy and now she's on HRT and she's ten years old."

"Marianne's in the same boat."

"Okay. Perhaps I'm over-identifying because of the testes being removed. You have to expect a man to get hung up about that." He managed a smile. "I explained it to her like an appendix. Something you have that you don't need."

"She's a very pretty little girl. And cheerful. Don't underestimate how your view of her shapes her self-esteem. She needs a good father figure if she's going to relate well to men."

I will be that good father, Bob thought. *I will spend whatever it takes and sacrifice whatever it takes to give her a normal life.*

"Janice again?" Gina called from the kitchen when he came in. He could hear

Vicky playing her flute upstairs.

"Yes," he said, offering nothing more.

"Thought so," Gina said, and the conversation died.

#

Seventeen years exactly.

"Happy Birthday Granddaughter." An embossed foil card, no feminine froth, with a vid chip that plays a mountain landscape when you pick it up. "Many happy returns, Vicky. From Gran." Nothing more.

The Hickson matriarch had never found it easy to deal with Vicky. "She's much closer to her father," she'd declared. Bob decided it was a command rather than an observation. That suited him just fine. There was no reason why a man couldn't provide the emotional support a daughter needed. He was there to offer a sympathetic ear when Vicky was the only girl in class not able to brag about periods: he could just as easily identify with her first fears about not being able to bear children.

There was nothing Gina could offer that he couldn't. That might have been the reason behind the divorce.

Vicky lived with him now. She had grown up into the tall, striking glamour

typical – so some said – of CAIS girls. Her glossy brown hair reached her waist. Boys pestered her for dates. Bob exercised just a little more fatherly vigilance over her these days than most dads, but only a little. He wanted her to feel normal. Or at least as normal as a teenager could feel when she had surgeons discussing vaginal hypoplasia and the merits of Vechietti procedures over her head.

For a birthday treat he took her to the smartest restaurant in town. It was the first time she'd worn a formal cocktail outfit, and he gave her a corsage of a single magenta cattleya orchid.

It was almost a joke between them, orchids: an exotically feminine bloom from a masculine pseudo-bulb, even its generic name derived from the Greek for testicle. Bob hadn't known a thing about orchids until he'd seen the image in AIS support literature, and now he knew plenty about both.

The cattleya's fragrance filled the space between them as they chose from an eclectic wine list. Bob caught himself searching the menu for something with a good calcium content for her, something to ward off the osteoporosis AIS girls could be prone to. He stopped himself. She was old enough now to manage her condition herself.

"This is ever so posh," Vicky said. "I've never seen so much crystal in my life."

Bob leaned towards her across the real damask tablecloth. "I'll let you into a secret, sweetheart – neither have I." Father and daughter giggled. He looked up and caught the waiter's unfathomable eye. "We're still undecided," he said, wondering if the man was judging them. "But we'll have a half-bottle of the Riquewihr Pinot Gris while we're making up our minds."

It was more a spectacle than a meal. Vicky appeared to be enjoying it. She had always been a controlled person, not much given to displays, but he could tell she was pleased. They talked about her university choices and short-term stuff and marvelled at after-dinner chocolate confections like Faberge eggs. Later they walked through the town centre.

People were spilling out of the theatre and heading towards bars and restaurants, a second shift. An older couple with two small children — grandchildren, Bob assumed, although that was by no means certain these days — crossed their path.

"I won't be able to give you those," Vicky said suddenly.

"What?"

"Grandchildren."

"You mustn't even think that." Bob stopped her in her tracks: she was as

tall as he was now. "I mean it. It's nothing. I don't want you to lose a second's sleep over that, do you understand?"

"You know – "

"Hey, I have everything I could possibly want."

They dropped the subject as if by an unspoken signal and carried on past the riverside walk. It was a busy evening. People milled around.

"Oh, Bob," said a voice.

It was a business associate, a man he hadn't seen in years. He couldn't put a name to him, but the face reminded him of a project, and he returned a non-committal greeting.

"So there's life in you yet, eh, Bob?" the man said. He was smiling at Vicky.

It took Bob a couple of seconds to wring the meaning from that. He realised he was frowning. "This is my daughter," he said. "My daughter Vicky."

The man's expression crumpled into embarrassment. "I'm

sorry, Bob. She's just – well, I forgot how long it's been. She's a lovely girl."

Bob couldn't recall later how the exchange ended, but it was hurried and flustered. All he remembered – and remembered for years after – was that a relative stranger had been struck by his daughter's beauty.

A lovely girl. Yes, she was.

#

Twenty-five years and ten months. A sheet designed to look like an old-fashioned telegram. "CONGRATULATIONS VICKY. I KNEW YOU WOULD DO IT. YOUNG ENTREPRENEUR OF THE YEAR! LOVE DAD."

#

Twenty-six years and two months. Silver bells and horseshoes embossed on ivory. Some cards never change." On your wedding, dear daughter. Congratulations again, sweetheart. I wish you every happiness with Marc. With love from Dad."

The line from Canada was uncharacteristically poor. Bob reloaded the number a few times but the picture was still snow-stormed and Vicky's voice crackled. He would have to get a better link installed.

"You don't have to go through with this."

"I want to." Her hair was shoulder-length now, more business-like than princess. "I want to more than anything."

"Not for me, love. Please."

"Marc's over the moon about the idea."

"Vicky, please."

"There's nothing to worry about. Reproduction technology has improved enormously since I was born. We can guarantee so much more."

"You're thinking about gestation by donor, aren't you?"

"You know the problem with surrogacy. It's not the best

solution."

"Even so, these women are in comas."

"They've left living wills. What's the difference between leaving your organs for tissue culture and donating time in your uterus? They don't even have to die to help people."

"I don't know. We crossed a line a long time ago. Maybe I shouldn't feel uncomfortable with it."

Vicky shimmered on screen for a second, and he thought he'd lost the link. He tapped the pad to locate a stronger signal. "We have the embryo. A boy. And we have had everything, I mean everything, checked out." She smiled that anxious and hopeful smile that always told him she was looking for his approval. "Wouldn't you love a grandson, dad?"

Bob paused. He could have remarried and had more children. He could have adopted. He could have done a great many things, but he had chosen to invest all in his barren daughter.

But she wasn't barren now. The next generation of doctors had managed to place her genetic material in a donor ovum stripped of its owner's inheritance, and fertilise it with Marc Peraud's sperm. Now they were offering to take the embryo out of storage and implant it in a woman who hadn't regained consciousness after an accident. It seemed monstrous to Bob and he didn't know why, not rationally anyway. Once over that line of medical intervention, what was normal in procreation any more? Yes, he would have loved a grandson. He could see Vicky wanted that too.

"Darling, go ahead. Whatever you need." Bob wished he had used a voice-line: could she see his anxiety at her end? "I said I'd do whatever it took to give you a normal life. Go ahead. You deserve it. And give my love to Marc."

"I'm so proud of you, dad," she said. "Maybe we can let him have the Fraser surname, seeing as you're the last – "

"No need," Bob said. "No need at all."

#

Thirty-seven years and four months. A plain card. Understated wreath, a non-denominational religious feel to the discreet gilding. "With deepest sympathy. Vicky, I was so sorry to hear about your Dad. He loved you and the kids so much, and he was a wonderful friend to me. Thinking of you. Janice Thomas."

"Vicky, are you coming down?" Marc was one of those men who couldn't bring themselves to shout. He whispered loudly and theatrically. Vicky smiled and tucked the envelope under her arm, intent on resuming her browsing later once the dinner guests had gone.

"I'm coming," she called.

Marc had set the dining room with cattleyas, cymbidiums and odontoglossums in full bloom from the orchid house. Vicky had done well out of propagating them for the cut-flower trade, but they had never become commonplace for her. She loved them. Simon was wandering from bloom to bloom like a demented bee, sniffing hard.

"Mum, they don't all smell strong, do they?" he said.

"Smell strongly, love," she corrected. "No, some orchids aren't fragrant at all. But aren't they lovely?"

"Gran'pa liked them, didn't he?"

Vicky stood beside her son and admired the almost crystalline glitter of the palest of apricot cymbidiums, spotted with carmine at its throat. It was her finest: she'd bred it herself and propagated it from a meristem. It was the current sensation in floristry.

As its breeder she'd been entitled to name it. She had registered it as *Robert Fraser*.

"Yes,' she said. "Gran'pa loved orchids very much."

###

ALSO BY KAREN TRAVISS:

RINGER
Going Grey

WESS'HAR WARS
City of Pearl
Crossing the Line
The World Before
Matriarch
Ally
Judge

HALO
Glasslands
The Thursday War
Mortal Dictata

GEARS OF WAR
Aspho Fields
Jacinto's Remnant
Anvil Gate
Coalition's End
The Slab

STAR WARS: REPUBLIC COMMANDO
Hard Contact
Triple Zero
True Colors
Order 66
Imperial Commando: 501st

STAR WARS
Bloodlines
Sacrifice
Revelation
The Clone Wars
No Prisoners

ABOUT THE AUTHOR

#1 *New York Times* best-selling novelist, scriptwriter and comics author Karen Traviss has received critical acclaim for her award-nominated Wess'har series, as well as regularly hitting the bestseller lists with her *Halo*, *Gears of War*, and *Star Wars* work. A former defence correspondent and TV and newspaper journalist, she lives in Wiltshire, England.

For more information on Karen's books and other work, or to contact her, visit www.karentraviss.com.

Printed in Great Britain
by Amazon